A Bit of Sugar

Deborah Wilson

Take reading
by the reins!

Debbie Wilson

First published by Dog Ear Publishing
4011 Vincennes Rd
Indianapolis, IN 46268
www.dogearpublishing.net

ISBN: 978-1-4575-4232-9

This book is printed on acid-free paper.

This book is a work of fiction. Places, events, and situations in this book are purely fictional and any resemblance to actual persons, living or dead, is coincidental.

Printed in the United States of America

Dedication

First and foremost, I want to thank my husband, James Wilson, for all the love and support he gave me through this journey. My three wonderful children who mean the world to me. To my parents for allowing me to follow my passion for horses. A special thanks to Dr. Patricia Kusik for her encouragement, without her this dream would have never been realized.

Chapter 1

Mrs. Tucker, the fourth grade teacher at Winslow Elementary School, asked everyone to pull out their copies of *Little House in the Big Woods* and follow along. As the students took turns reading, Laura Maynor became lost in her *own* story. She was riding the prettiest pony in town.

As Laura galloped up the hill, her thick, long blond hair, wrapped in a tight ponytail, moved in harmony with the real pony's tail. The countryside was filled with sunflowers at the peak of their beauty. Freshly fallen red and gold leaves lay under the majestic mature trees.

Migrating geese flew overhead in a perfect V formation. An eagle, perched in a gigantic oak tree, watched her every move. Laura leaned forward, urging her pony to go faster... If a grade could be given for daydreaming, she would have received an A+.

Laura had just reached the crest of the hill in her fantasy, when she was startled by the teacher's firm voice.

"Laura! Laura Maynor!" Mrs. Tucker scolded. "It's your turn to read!"

Laura tried to find her place in the book, but it was obvious to everyone that she hadn't been paying attention.

"Are you daydreaming again?" Mrs. Tucker asked loudly in front of the whole class.

Her classmates broke into heartless giggles. Laura's face turned fire-engine red as she tried desperately not to cry.

Sitting at her desk waiting for this horrible day to end, Laura chewed her nails nervously. She was anxious to go home, and there was some comfort knowing that her mom would be picking her up after school.

"Are you okay, Laura?" Rose, Laura's mom, asked her later, as Laura climbed into her seat and slammed the car door.

"No! It was the worst day ever! I hate school." Laura turned away from her mother as tears poured out of her hazel blue eyes. "I'm never going back!"

"What happened? Did those boys make fun of you again?" Rose handed her daughter a tissue. "Because if they did, we'll march right back into school and I'll straighten this out!"

"No, Mom! No one called me 'fat' today. I was confused when we were reading a book together, and when Mrs. Tucker called on me, I was lost. The whole class laughed at me."

"Were you daydreaming again, Laura? You need to pay attention in class," Rose insisted. "You only have a week of school left before summer break," she added as they drove home.

"I tried to pay attention Mom, but the book was about ponies." She sighed. "And I was thinking about having one of my own."

"Laura, I know you would love to have a pony, but it's a lot of responsibility. You need to do well in school—that is your first priority. We've talked about this before, and I still don't think you're ready."

With the tears stopping, Laura declared, "I know, Mom, but Pop-Pop said last week that I *am* ready and that he would help me. I heard you and Dad fighting about me having a pony. You're wrong! I am old enough! You're never, ever going to let me have one, are you?"

In the silence that followed, Rose tried to compose herself. "Laura, I'm sorry you heard us arguing, but please don't be rude to me. I will not tolerate you talking to me in that way."

"Yes, ma'am," Laura replied. "I'm sorry, but I still want a pony."

"Laura, that's enough talk about a pony, and please stop chewing your nails. I was thinking we could stop at

Eugene's Restaurant after church on Sunday and pick up ribs to take home. Doesn't that sound nice?"

Laura reluctantly nodded in agreement as she stared out the open window and felt the warm breeze blow across her face.

"Can you smile a little for me? Sunday is just two days away, and I can't wait to spend the whole day together with your dad. It will be nice having him home for the whole day."

* * *

After a long sermon at church that Sunday, Laura was riding home with her parents. She found herself gazing out of the car window staring at the clouds floating by, and she began to fantasize about winning the trophy at the Maryland State Fair. Pop-Pop had taken her there last year, and she had never seen anything more exciting. In this dream, she was riding a beautiful pony with a long flaxen mane and tail. The magnificent pony performed perfectly.

When all the riders and ponies lined up in the center of the ring, waiting to hear the judges' results, all of the other riders glared at Laura and her mount with envy. In her fantasy, Laura had just won the trophy, and the biggest smile stretched across her face.

Her dad saw her smile in the rearview mirror and chuckled to himself. "Laura, what are you thinking about?"

"Um, well, I was just thinking what it would be like to have my own pony."

Her dad grinned and laughed. "Why am I not surprised? Rose, why don't you tell Laura about the pony your dad gave you on your birthday?"

"Mom, is that the picture of the pony that you keep in your Bible along with my baby picture?"

"Yes, it is. When did you see that?"

"I was looking up a Bible verse for Sunday school when I saw it. Please tell me about him."

"All right," Rose said with a sigh. "His name was Trigger, and Pop-Pop had a cowboy bring him to my tenth birthday party for pony rides. He was the most well-mannered pony I had ever seen. All my friends took turns riding him, and he was so patient with them. There must have been fifteen kids from the neighborhood climbing on and off him. He would look around at each one, as if he was hoping one of them would be the last.

"I was the last one to get on—my dad said I had to wait to be courteous to my friends. I remember petting his nose as he turned around, and I noticed his deep red color. His coat was as shiny as a new penny. When I climbed on and went for my loop around the yard, I couldn't imagine how smooth he was. As the cowboy stopped the pony, he said, 'Happy birthday, Rose! This is your present from your mom and dad!' I almost fell off in disbelief." Rose stopped the story and felt a lump forming in her throat.

"What happened to him?" Laura asked intently.

"I'll finish the story another day. He was truly one of the best friends I have ever had."

There was silence in the car as they pulled into Eugene's Restaurant. Rose wiped the tear running down her face. "I'll be right back. Can you and Laura go over to the fruit stand and pick out a nice watermelon?"

"Yes. Come on, Laura, we have an assignment," John said, as they stepped out of a 1964 Buick sport wagon.

"Dad, have you heard that story before?"

"A long time ago, Mom–Mom told me about him."

"I was surprised to see Mommy cry in the car."

"I have only seen her cry a couple of times. When you were born, and when Pop-Pop had a heart attack. She was so scared he wasn't going to make it, and the stress of taking care of so many horses really took a toll on her."

Laura and John made their way back to the car. "We beat her!" John joked.

Just as they sat down, the car door opened, and the aroma of the ribs flooded in. "They smell so good! My mouth is watering!" John noted.

"Mine, too!" Laura added. "Mom, I wish I had a best friend like Trigger."

There was no response from Rose. Laura thought, *If I had my own pony, he would be my best friend, too.*

"Laura, where would we keep a pony?" John asked.

"At Pop-Pop's. His barn is empty. He told me he used to have almost a hundred horses, so one pony would be fine. I would love to go to the State Fair!

"Laura, you're right," Rose said. He did have a lot of horses at one time, but they demanded too much of his energy. He had to sell them after his heart attack. That's why I don't want him to have to take care of even one pony now. Can you understand that?"

"Yes, but I would help."

Rose smiled. "I know you would, but we don't live close enough for you to go there every day. Knowing your grandfather, he would even start getting more ponies. It took Mom-Mom and me years to talk him into selling the ones he had. It was such a sad day when the last horse left. Pop-Pop never really seemed happy after that, until you were born. He seemed like his old self again after holding you for the first time at the hospital. Do you remember the day he brought you the Breyer barn and horses?"

"Yes. That was so much fun!"

"He seemed like a kid again, sitting in the middle of the living room, making horse noises. He has a deep love for horses, and I think you get that from him. We will talk about a pony maybe next year, okay? That's enough pony talk for today."

"Yes, ma'am", Laura said with a sigh.

They sat down at the kitchen table to eat the delicious spare ribs. They were all laughing as they looked at each other with their faces smeared with barbecue sauce.

"What are you going to do now?" John asked his daughter.

"Go play with my toy horses."

"Can you make your bed first, after you wash up?" Rose asked, clearing the table.

Rose and John began to talk in the kitchen while she folded the laundry. "Rose, I don't want to start a fight over this, but Laura really wants a pony."

"I'm not going to argue about this anymore. Do you know Laura heard us fighting the other night?"

"I wish she hadn't, but I know her desire isn't going to go away. You loved your pony. Don't you want Laura to have that, too?"

"John, I know how much she wants a pony. It's just so expensive, and there could be a lot of heartache. I don't want her to feel that kind of hurt." Rose seemed lost in thought, as, silence filled the room. She went to get more laundry.

She returned moments later with a determined look on her face. "I've been thinking about this, John, and I think she should start riding lessons."

John smiled. "I think that's a great idea!"

"That way we will know if she really will stick with it. Remember when she was doing dance, and I got her that fancy tutu and she never even put it on?"

"Rose, Laura never actually wanted to dance. That was your idea. I told you when you bought that tutu that she would never wear it."

Rose shook her head and glared at her husband. Then her expression relaxed. "Why don't you call my dad and see if he has any ideas about where to go for lessons?"

Laura's grandparents were finishing lunch when the phone rang.

"Hello," Pop-Pop said in his deep voice.

"Hey, Pop. It's John. Are you busy?"

"Maybe just a little!" Pop-Pop chuckled.

"Well, Rose and I were talking, and we think Laura is ready to start taking riding lessons."

Pop-Pop smiled. "She should have started years ago, John. Is Rose really okay with this?"

"Yes, it was her idea, after she refused to consider buying Laura a pony."

"She is so stubborn. I'll call an old friend of mine."

"Thanks. If you talk to Laura, don't say anything; it's a surprise!"

"I will call you back after I talk to Mrs. Taylor," Pop-Pop said quickly and then hung up the phone. He got up and went to his study. "Virginia," he shouted moments later, "where's the phone book with all my numbers?"

Mom-Mom finished drying her hands with a dish towel and followed after him. "What's all the fuss about?"

"John called, and they want Laura to start taking riding lessons, but I can't find my phone book."

"Calm down, it's right here," she said, retrieving it from under a pile of papers on his desk. "Here you go. Are you going to call Hadley Farm? Is Mrs. Taylor still teaching?"

"I hope so. She is the best person I can think of. We just need to buy a pony let Rose deal with it."

"Jack, you need to be happy that Rose is willing to let her ride. One thing at a time!" she said, opening the screen door. "I'm going out to plant my last row of corn for this year."

"I am happy about the lessons, but Laura needs her own pony," Pop-Pop said with conviction, as he thumbed quickly through the book.

"Oh good—here it is. Okay, I'll make this call and then come and help you." Then he thought to himself, *I am going to get her the nicest pony ever!*

Chapter 2

Mrs. Taylor had just returned from the barn after feeding the ponies, when she heard the phone ring. She quickly took off her muddy barn boots off and ran to the phone. "Hello, hello," she said, hoping she hadn't missed the call.

"Mrs. Taylor, this is Jack Anderson."

"Well, it's certainly good to hear your voice! It's been a long time."

Mrs. Taylor and Pop-Pop had known each other for years. He had purchased a few ponies from her in the past.

"I am looking for a pony for my granddaughter Laura. She is nine years old and all she thinks about are ponies."

"Reminds me of your daughter. I am sure we can find something for her. Let me look at my calendar." After a pause, Mrs. Taylor continued, "I could meet you this Saturday after lunch, or late in the morning on Sunday."

"We will be there Saturday. When you see Laura, be aware that she thinks she's just getting a lesson."

"I won't say a word. See you Saturday afternoon."

Pop-Pop hung up the phone and went upstairs to his sock drawer. He had a sock filled with cash that he called his "play money," but he had never spent it. Mom-Mom knew about it, but she always pretended not to see it. "Let's see how much is here," Pop-Pop said aloud to himself as he unfolded and counted the hidden bills... "$420...$425."

"That should be enough." He was stashing his sock away when he noticed Mom-Mom in the doorway.

"I know what you're up to," Virginia said as she sat on the edge the bed.

"It's not fair to make Laura suffer for a mistake I made twenty years ago. Why shouldn't she have *her* dreams come true?"

"Jack, it was an honest mistake. Rose doesn't blame you. She just doesn't want Laura to get hurt."

He lowered his head and continued, "I need to call John."

"Let's ride up to their house, and I can give Laura the crocheted blanket I fixed for her."

"That sounds good. I'll go call him now."

"John, Laura's riding lesson is scheduled for Saturday around one o'clock, at Hadley Farm," Pop-Pop said.

"That's not going to work. This Saturday morning we are going crabbing. We leave at five a.m. and will be gone for the entire day. Laura has been looking forward to this trip for weeks. Is there any way we could go on Sunday after church?"

"I forgot about your crabbing trip. I will call her back and schedule the lesson for eleven on Sunday. Are you going to be home now? We were going to stop by for a little while."

"Yes, we'll be here all day."

The doorbell rang and startled Rose, who was running the vacuum cleaner. "Come in. John said you might stop by." She looked at her father. "John and Laura are in the backyard playing catch, if you want to go visit with them."

Jack smiled and quickly made his way to the backyard.

"Here's the blanket I fixed for Laura," Mom-Mom said, handing it to Rose. "It should be fine now. Let's go put it on Laura's bed."

"Thanks, Mom, she does love this blanket." Rose led the way to Laura's room.

"I heard you've agreed to let Laura take riding lessons, Rose. I'm glad you changed your mind."

"I know her desire will never go away. I don't think I had a choice."

"Rose, you need to reconsider letting her have her own pony. I loved watching you with Trigger. Do you remember all the things you did with him? It was all I could do to get you to come inside and not sleep in the barn with him."

"Mom, I don't want to talk about this."

"Rose, your father has never forgiven himself for not fixing the latch on the stallion's door. He had planned to fix it after breakfast, but by then it was too late."

"Please stop!" Rose begged. Her lower lip was quivering.

"No, you're going to listen to this, her mother insisted. After he found Trigger so badly injured, he was devastated. He would have spent all the money in the world to fix him, but there was no hope. You need to understand how much this has affected him, and your not letting Laura have a pony only makes it worse. I would not trade the smile I saw on your face when you rode him, even knowing what would happen. Life is about happiness *and* loss. If you would let your dad buy her a pony, it would help him forgive himself. Please, Rose, give your dad this. He needs a purpose, a reason to get out of bed in the morning. We can handle taking care of one pony."

"I never realized how much it upset him. He went and bought me another pony the next day."

"He was trying to fix it, and that was the only way he thought he could. He wasn't trying to replace Trigger. He thought a new pony might have helped you get over him. You never even went down to see him. Every day he took care of that pony. It broke his heart."

"I couldn't imagine going into the barn and not hearing Trigger whinnying when he saw me. I was never angry at Daddy. I never wanted him to feel this way. I just couldn't get close to another pony."

"Rose, you never tried, so please let Laura experience the type of joy you had with Trigger, and if there's a loss, we will handle it then."

Remembering how she lost Trigger, Rose said, "I just wanted to say good-bye to my friend. Why wouldn't you let me go to the barn? I needed to be there for Trigger. He was always there for me. Then I heard the gunshot, and I knew I would never see him again...."

"Rose, you were so young we thought it was best that you didn't see him so badly hurt. We did what we thought was best. Maybe having seen him would have given you closure. I wanted to protect you, just like you are trying to protect Laura now. The difference is that you won't let Laura have the good thing, because you are trying to protect from a possible bad thing. You know the right thing to do, and I hope you can let Laura have the chance to let her dreams come true. Get yourself together, and dry your tears. I love you!" Mom-Mom leaned forward and kissed Rose on the head. Then she left and went to the kitchen.

"Rose," John called, sometime later, "your parents are leaving, do you want to say good-bye?"

"Yes!" Rose answered, not realizing how long she had been sitting in Laura's bedroom, lost in thought, and tightly holding on to the blanket, when she heard John. Rose quickly ran downstairs and met Laura coming in from outside. "Give Mom-Mom a hug, they are leaving."

Laura rushed through the door to say good-bye, and John and Jack walked over to see Rose.

"Dad I've been thinking..." Rose whispered in her father's ear. "We should buy Laura a pony." Then she gave him a hug.

"Really?" Jack smiled and wrapped his arms around Rose. "Thank-you! I want to buy the pony for her. I've been saving for this day for a while."

"*Shh!* Don't let Laura hear us," Rose insisted. "We will help with the money too."

Mom-Mom saw the smile on Pop-Pops face and knew Rose had listened to her. With everyone beaming, Mom-Mom and Pop-Pop headed home.

Rose and Laura cleaned and dried the dinner dishes and put them away. By now, it was almost time for the family to watch their favorite weekly television show.

"Laura," Rose said, "go take a shower. I'll make the popcorn."

"Yes, ma'am!" Laura said as she hurried off.

"What changed your mind about getting Laura a pony?" John asked.

"My mother did. We had a long talk and it really helped me see how happy it would make Laura."

"I'm glad you changed your mind. I think all of us will enjoy having a pony. How much money do you think we'll need?"

"I really don't know, maybe $600? She's going to need a saddle and a helmet, too."

"Let's see, I'll get a notepad," John said as he opened the office desk in the corner of the kitchen. "Okay, how much for a tack?"

"Maybe a hundred dollars, and then let's figure on six hundred for the pony, and thirty dollars for feed and hay. So seven hundred and thirty dollars should be enough to start."

John gave a look of surprise and scratched his head. "Are you okay if your parents help? That's a little more than I thought."

"Yes. I think they would be insulted if we didn't let them."

Just then, Laura walked into the kitchen. "Let's go, the show's starting!"

"Okay, Miss Bossy Pants," John answered as he chased her into the living room.

Rose quickly hid the notepad and grabbed the popcorn. The family sat on the plaid couch snuggled up together, under the blanket Mom-Mom had just repaired. As they reached for the popcorn, Rose and John looked at each other lovingly and smiled. They knew how different things would be the same time next week.

Chapter 3

After dinner on Friday night, John and Laura sat side by side in the backyard on two empty upside-down buckets, preparing for the next morning's crabbing adventure. "I love being on the water early in the morning and watching the sun come up, don't you?" John Maynor asked his daughter as he finished cutting the rope. "It was a long week at work."

"It was a long week at school, too!"

"Yes, but you'll be finished fourth grade soon!" He smiled at his daughter. "Laura, I want you to tie the chicken necks on the rope about every ten feet."

"How long is this rope, Dad?"

"About four hundred feet from buoy to buoy. That's about average for a trout line."

"This is disgusting!" Laura said, as she got a whiff of the rotting chicken necks. She crinkled her nose and turned her head away, trying not to gag. "This smells like the dead skunk we saw when we went hiking."

"I don't think it's that bad!" John laughed. "If it makes you sick, I can do it."

"No, I'm okay! I'm so excited to go crabbing. It's all I could think about this week. It's so cool you have off all day on a Saturday!"

"I am excited, too! Does that mean that you weren't dreaming about ponies this week? I always thought you would make a great commercial crabber!"

"Dad... You must be kidding me!" Laura's eyes bulged. "I am going to be a horse trainer! These chicken necks are so slimy, I can barely hold on to them."

"You'd better get cleaned up and head off to bed. Four o'clock in the morning will be here sooner than you think. I'll finish the rest of the line."

"Why do we have to leave so early?"

"The best time to catch crabs is when the high tide is heading out, and in June, that's normally before noon."

They were on the Chesapeake Bay promptly at 5:00 a.m. As they raced across the waves to their destination, Laura sat in the front of the bouncing boat holding a line tied to the shiny cleat. She closed her eyes and dreamed of jumping her champion pony over four foot jumps all in a row. John watched Laura, and he knew she wasn't on the water anymore, but in a large meadow somewhere, riding.

That afternoon, when they returned home, Rose met them in the driveway. "How many did you catch?"

"Almost four dozen!" Laura beamed. "It was a great day."

"I'm going to clean the boat off," John said, "and then we will steam the crabs."

"There should be enough left over that I can make crab soup," Rose said excitedly. "I picked up some fresh vegetables at the farmer's market today."

"Mom, your crab soup is the best!"

"Thank you! You need to go take a shower. You smell like a dead fish!"

"Do I have to?" Laura asked.

"Yes, you do, young lady! Now off you go." Rose watched Laura slowly walk to the house.

"John, my dad called Mrs. Taylor today to confirm our appointment for tomorrow. Everything is set."

"I'm so excited," John said, and he leaned forward to give Rose a kiss.

Rose stepped back and laughed." You smell worse than Laura!"

"I'll finish washing the boat and be in to clean up." He chuckled.

Rose headed in to the garage to check on how soon the crabs would be finished. "Are they ready?"

"Not yet," Laura said. "I've set a timer. In ten minutes, they'll be finished. Dad said they take twenty-eight minutes once they start to steam."

John came back into the garage. "The newspaper is down on the table, the crab mallets are out, and we are ready to eat," he said.

"Be careful, Laura. They are very hot," he said as he placed a steaming pile of crabs on the table along with the piping hot corn on the cob. "Do you remember how to open them?"

"Not really," Laura said, looking up at her father.

"Flip the crab over and pull the apron up, then put your thumb between the shell and the body of the crab, and pull it off," John instructed.

"I think I got it." Laura exclaimed as the crab came apart.

"Now clean out the lungs, or the 'devils,' but don't eat them, and then crack it in half." He watched Laura's progress. "Good job. Now let's crack those claws open. Grab a mallet and hold on to the claw. Wait, let me show you," he said, as he reached for the butter knife, and placed it right below the pinchers of the claw. Holding the knife steady with one hand, he used the other to hit the knife with the mallet, splitting the hard shell and exposing the juicy white meat.

"Now all you have to do is pull it out, and eat it. Laura, you try."

Laura took the hammer in her right hand, and with all her might banged the claw. It darted unexpectedly through the air.

"Watch out, Mom!"

Rose ducked as she stepped out of the back door. "That was close."

"Sorry, Mom. I guess I hit it too hard." Laura smiled and tried not to giggle.

"That's okay, honey. We'd better hurry along and start picking the crabs, so I have time to make the crab soup for tomorrow."

* * *

The Sunday sermon was shorter than usual. "We all must remember God has a plan, and we need to learn how to accept things we have no control over. We must find peace in our hearts and trust in God. Amen." And with that, Pastor Grove concluded his talk.

Laura was surprised later, when she actually remembered what the pastor had said.

"You shouldn't race in a parking lot." Rose scolded John and Laura, who were running for the car.

"Can I get a root beer when we stop to pick up the ribs?" Laura asked.

"Not today. We can't get ribs this week," John answered.

"Why not? I really want them!"

"We have a stop to make on the way home. It won't take long." Rose explained. "When we get home, we'll have the crab soup."

"Oh that's right, I can't wait!"

Laura felt the car slow down and start to turn on to a dirt driveway. The sign in the middle of the V-shaped driveway read HADLEY FARM. Laura's confusion turned to delight as the car drove down the dirt lane.

The trees seemed like they touched the clouds, they were so tall. Their branches shaded the entire width of the lane. Post and rail fence ran the entire length. There were lush green pastures, as far as you could see, with ponies scattered throughout the fields.

"What are we doing here?"

"This is our stop," John said.

Just then, Laura saw Mom-Mom and Pop-Pop, waiting under the huge old oak tree. John parked the car next to Pop-Pop's truck, and Laura jumped out and ran over to her grandparents. She gave them a hug as tightly as she could.

"What are you doing here?" she asked.

"Well…we scheduled a riding lesson for you, because I heard your teacher was really proud of you this quarter and we are, too!" Pop-Pop explained.

"Really? Oh my gosh, I can't believe it! Where do I go?"

"Slow down, Laura, you need to change your clothes first," Rose said. "I have play clothes for you in the back of the car. Hop in the backseat and you can change."

"We'll wait over here while you change, sweetie," Mom-Mom said.

Laura changed as fast as she could and then rejoined them. Together, they headed toward the quaint red barn. Ponies looked out from fences on both sides of the path. Laura found it difficult to keep up with the family. She couldn't stop staring at their big brown eyes gazing right back at her.

Mrs. Taylor stood by the barn with her six beloved dogs and a battered bucket in her overworked hand. Her hair was as white as snow, and her sundress seemed to be dancing in the breeze. Her lovely worn face seemed to reflect all her years of farm life. She was barely as tall as the fence post she was standing beside.

Pop-Pop shook Mrs. Taylor's hand and proceeded to introduce his family.

"Mrs. Taylor, do you remember Virginia and Rose?"

"Of course. It's nice to see you again, Virginia." She leaned forward to shake her hand. "And how could I forget one of the most talented riders I've ever met? How have you been, Rose?"

"It's good to see you, Mrs. Taylor. This is my husband, John, and our daughter, Laura."

"Nice to meet you, young lady. I've heard you are quite the pony lover. You sound just like your mom."

"Yes, ma'am. I really do love ponies," Laura replied, almost speechless.

"Well, today you're going to ride two different ponies for your lesson. I will meet you in the barn after I feed the old stallion. My granddaughter, Jodi, is in the barn tacking them up right now."

"I can't believe I am going to ride today!" Laura exclaimed.

"Laura, why don't you and Pop-Pop go to the barn, and I'll show your dad and Mom-Mom around the farm," Rose offered.

They walked into the little red barn and saw four eyes peering back at them through the wooden boards of the stalls. There were two ponies in stalls peeking out, trying to see who was there. Laura had found her heaven, and the smell of hay, grain, and ponies stopped her in her tracks.

Jodi came out of the tiny room that they used to store tack. She was carrying a bucket filled with brushes, and she moved in a very confident way.

"Hi, I'm Jodi. You must be Laura. Here are some brushes. You can brush Pinocchio. He's the one in the stall behind you. I'll start tacking up Rags."

"Hi, Jodi, I'm Laura's granddad, Jack Anderson."

"Hello, Mr. Anderson. Do you want to wait by the ring while she tacks up the pony?" Jodi suggested with her hand on her hip.

"No, thank you. I'll stay with Laura. This is her first time." Pop-Pop shook his head. "Which one is Pinocchio?"

"Oh, I thought you had ponies. You've never ridden before?" Jodi asked sarcastically.

"No, I haven't," Laura answered as she started to chew her nails.

"I had ponies many years ago. Which one is Pinocchio?" Pop-Pop asked again, with irritation.

"He's the one right behind you," Jodi answered. She held her nose in the air as she headed into Rag's stall.

"Don't let her bother you. She's just jealous," Pop-Pop whispered in Laura's ear.

"Why is she jealous of me?" Laura whispered.

"We'll talk about that later. Come on, I want you to enjoy yourself today."

Laura walked into the stall, trying not to trip on the straw bedding, which came up to her knees. She approached Pinocchio, letting him smell her hand. She could feel his warm breath blow across her hand. Laura then went on to run her hands along his neck and down his back. As Pop-Pop watched her, he thought, *She looks like she's been around ponies her whole life.*

"I've never seen a pony this color before. What do you call it?" Laura asked.

"It's referred to as silver dapple, and it's kind of a mousy color. I bet after a bath his mane and tail would shine like silver. I think he must be around ten and a half hands."

"What's a hand?"

"Horses and ponies are measured in hands. There are four inches to each hand, so I guess he's about forty-two inches tall."

Mrs. Taylor entered the barn. "Sorry I took so long. My poor old stallion has no teeth left. I have to soak his food for hours. It's tough getting old. I see you have met

Pinocchio. He's a good boy, a bit green, I think. Jodi has ridden him about fifteen times? Isn't that right, Jodi?"

"Yes, Gram," Jodi replied.

"He's only six, and some of these thick-headed Shetlands aren't really well broke till they are around eight, but he's a quick learner. Have you met the other pony? He just arrived late last week from the eastern shore of Maryland," Mrs. Taylor said. "His name is Hadley Ragged Robin. We call him Rags. He is twelve years old, eleven hands tall, and has a long show record. In fact, he has won the Maryland state trophy three times with three different girls. Laura, you can go in the stall with him."

"Be careful, Laura. He just nipped at me," Jodi announced.

"Jodi, tack up Pinocchio, and that's enough from you. Laura, he did no such thing. He wouldn't hurt a fly," Mrs. Taylor said, shaking her head in disgust.

"Yes, ma'am," Jodi quickly replied. She rolled her eyes as she headed into the tack room.

"Come on, Laura," Pop-Pop encouraged her. "He looks very sweet."

Rags was a deep red chestnut, with a white blaze that ran down the middle of his dished face. His mane had silver highlights, and his forelock was as long as his blaze, almost touching his nose. His tail, which dragged the ground, gave him a royal appearance. Rags knew he was special, having always had a little girl who cared for and loved him.

Laura walked into the stall, but instead of examining him as she did Pinocchio, she was a little hesitant after the report Jodi had given. Soon she realized how agreeable he was. She gave him a hug, wrapping her arms tightly around his neck and burying her nose in his mane. It was the most soothing scent she had ever smelled.

Pop-Pop walked into the stall to take a closer look. He moved his hand all over Rags, checking for any lumps or bumps that could cause a problem. He thought to himself, *This is one of the nicest ponies I have ever seen!*

Chapter 4

Rose and Mom-Mom arrived at the barn just in time to see Laura in the stall hugging Rags. They looked at each other with delight, hoping they were looking at Laura's new pony.

"They remind me of how you looked the day you got Trigger," Mom-Mom said to Rose. "It was one of the most memorable days in my life."

"Would you like to take Rags for a walk while Jodi finishes up?" Mrs. Taylor asked Laura, as Jodi walked by, staring at her.

"Yes!" Laura exclaimed.

Mrs. Taylor showed Laura the correct way to lead a pony. "You always want the pony on your right side. Hold your right hand close to the halter, with the extra lead rope in your left hand. Make sure you never wrap the lead rope around your hand."

"What do you think of the ponies, Pop-Pop?" John asked, watching Laura and Mom-Mom.

"I think Rags is the one for her, but we should see her ride both of them."

Mrs. Taylor came out of the barn and said, "Don't mean to interrupt, but Rags is one of the best ponies I have ever owned. He has been owned by three different girls, all who have outgrown him, and then he comes back to me to sell to the next child. All my ponies are sold with a contract, and in the contract the owner must notify me when they are going to sell the pony. This ensures the pony's best interests are taken care of, making sure it never ends up in a bad situation. Rags is so special, I make sure he comes back to my farm to be sold, and I personally meet the buyers."

"Are these the only two broke ponies you have now?" Pop-Pop inquired.

"Yes, it's unusual for me to have two riding ponies for sale at the same time. It's hard for me to keep up with the demand. Most of my ponies are sold as soon as they are weaned from the mothers, around five months old."

Pop-Pop asked, "What are you asking for each of them?"

"I am asking $950 for Rags, and $450 for Pinocchio," Mrs. Taylor answered.

Pop-Pop thought, *That's more than I expected.* "Can she ride both of them?" he asked.

"Yes. I'll tell Jodi to bring Pinocchio and Rags's bridles. Rose, will you go get Laura?"

"Does Rags remind you of somebody?" she asked Mrs. Taylor.

"He sure does. I'll go get them. Trigger was an outstanding pony. I was so sorry to hear about what happened to him," she added, as she headed to the barn.

Rose shook her head in agreement trying not to remember that horrid day. She turned and quickly left to get Laura.

"Both ponies are selling for more than Rose and I had discussed," John said.

"I'm shocked!" Pop-Pop said. "I didn't realize how much prices have gone up. I have $425."

"I think Rose and I can come up with the extra $500. Business has been good this month. I think we will be fine. But she may have to wait a little while for a tack."

Jodi was leading Pinocchio to the ring, as Laura followed with Rags.

"Jodi, get Rags and I'll have Laura ride Pinocchio first," Mrs. Taylor said. "Put his bridle on and hack him around the ring."

"Gram, can I jump Rags a little?"

"No. Not after the stunt you pulled earlier," Mrs. Taylor said. "Laura, come into the middle of the ring and put this helmet on."

Laura quickly ran over to Mrs. Taylor. "No running around the ponies!"

Laura stopped dead in her tracks and began to chew her nails.

"It's okay. You could just spook them," Mrs. Taylor explained. "Now, come on and put this helmet on."

Laura slowly walked toward Mrs. Taylor, when she was startled by Jodi and Rags trotting right behind her.

"Jodi, you know better." Mrs. Taylor scolded as she placed the helmet on Laura's head. "This helmet seems to fit. Is it too tight?"

"No. It feels perfect."

"Now, let's check your stirrup length. Put the stirrup in your armpit and reach for the end of the leather, where it connects to the saddle."

Laura was feeling a little clumsy and out of sorts as she stretched her fingertips toward the saddle.

"They seem a little long. I'll shorten the leathers about two holes. Mrs. Taylor quickly made all of the adjustments then said to Laura, "You should always check your girth before you get on. I already did, but you're the one riding. Can you put your fingers between the pony's side and the string girth?"

Laura took her fingers and easily put her whole hand underneath the girth. "It seems loose to me."

"You are right. Good job. You passed your first test. Look at Jodi. She loves riding Rags, and she doesn't get to ride many well-broke ponies."

"Why?"

"They don't stay around long. They are usually sold so fast she only gets to ride them a couple of times."

"Is Rags for sale?" Laura quickly asked.

"Everything's for sale, but don't worry about that now. Let's get you on this pony. I want you to face the saddle on his left side. Now, give me your left leg, and when I count to three, swing your right leg over the saddle: one, two, and three."

Laura found herself sitting on a pony for the first time. Pinocchio was not very patient, and he abruptly began to walk off before Laura was ready. Off she fell onto the hot sand.

She quickly stood up and brushed the sand off, ready to try again. Her dad started to run over to her, when he realized she was fine.

Jodi, watching the fall, thought to herself, *Oh, this is going to be fun!*

"Are you okay?" Mrs. Taylor asked, as she reprimanded the naughty pony.

"I'm fine. Can I try again?"

"Yes, but let's start with Rags first. I think Pinocchio may need some more training before you ride him again. Congratulations! I always tell my students they need to fall off seven times to be a good rider! You're well on your way."

"I'll be a good rider soon!" Laura giggled as she adjusted her helmet.

"Jodi, come over here. Take Pinocchio and let Laura ride Rags," Mrs. Taylor said.

"Okay, but she'd better be careful. Rags just spooked at the cow in the field next to the barn," Jodi announced.

"I think he will do just fine, young lady."

"Is Rags scared of cows?" Laura asked.

"No, Jodi's scared that she won't be able to ride him anymore," Mrs. Taylor explained.

Mom-Mom said proudly, "If falling off the minute she got on doesn't discourage her, nothing will."

"I was a little concerned at first, but she seems unscratched," Rose added.

"That Jodi is a little spitfire," Pop-Pop said. "Laura is getting on Rags now."

"One, two, and three, and up you go!" Mrs. Taylor ordered.

This time she sat motionless, as Mrs. Taylor put her feet in the stirrups and showed her how to hold her reins.

"Now, when you want him to move forward, give him a nudge or a kick with your heels, but remember to always keep your heels down and your toes toward the sky. When you want to stop, sit up nice and tall and pull gently on your reins and he will halt. To turn right, pull your right hand with the reins toward your knee, and the same for the left side. Got it?"

"Yes, ma'am," Laura quickly answered, as she had been waiting her whole life for this moment. "Are you sure he's okay around the cow?"

"Yes, I guarantee he won't care about the cow!" Mrs. Taylor responded as she glared at Jodi, who had just started to ride Pinocchio. "Well then, off you go."

"By myself?"

"Yes, make a figure eight and then come back to see me!"

Laura gave Rags a nudge with her heels, and nothing happened. She gave him a light kick, and he obediently began to walk forward, waiting for his cues.

Mrs. Taylor walked toward the family, who was sitting quietly under the partially shaded viewing area.

"I think everyone should be impressed with her. I know I am! She is amazing and fearless. What are your thoughts on Rags? I think it's a perfect match!"

"Well, to be honest, his price was more than we were prepared to spend," Pop-Pop answered.

"I know the prices are up from years ago, but with more children taking riding lessons, it has driven the prices up. I am sure both ponies will be sold within a couple of weeks," Mrs. Taylor said.

"I would love for her to have a Hadley pony. Can we call you in the morning? That will give us a chance to figure out the money," Pop-Pop said.

"That's fine. No one else is coming by today, so I will hear from you in the morning."

"Yes, I will call you in the morning," Pop-Pop said. "Jodi is quite a talented rider herself."

"Thank-you. She is a good rider, but I'm afraid she won't stick with it. I look forward to hearing from you in the morning. Well, I'd better get back to the lesson."

Mrs. Taylor went in the middle of the ring and started an intense conversation with Jodi. When Laura and Rags passed in front of the viewing area, she smiled proudly at her family.

"You look great, Laura!" Pop-Pop shouted.

"Rags is perfect!!" Laura exclaimed. "Did you know he's for sale?"

"Yes, Mrs. Taylor mentioned that. You'd better pay attention to your lesson, so you don't miss anything," Pop-Pop said.

"But, Pop-Pop, I'm in love!" Laura begged.

"Okay, we'll talk later!"

"Laura, I want you to work on trotting Rags," Mrs. Taylor instructed. "Walk to the end of the ring standing up and down as he walks. When you get to the end of the ring, turn and trot to me going up and down. That is called 'posting.'"

Laura turned Rags and headed toward the end of the ring, feeling a bit anxious. They made the turn, and she squeezed Rags with her heels and he began to trot.

"Perfect job, Laura! You're a natural." Mrs. Taylor smiled. "You are very good at posting. Let's do that one more time, and then your lesson will be over."

"Gram, can I please jump Pinocchio?" Jodi pleaded.

"No, not today. You have to head home soon. Did you see how well Laura did with Rags?"

"No, I wasn't watching. I am done. Can you put Pinocchio away? I don't want to be late for my Four-H meeting," Jodi announced.

"Yes, I will, but your attitude needs to change before you ride again. Do you understand?"

Jodi nodded in agreement, jumped off, and ran to her house on the other side of the farm.

"Come over here, Laura, and dismount. Take both feet out of the stirrups and lean forward. Now, swing your right leg over and slide down. Did you enjoy your first lesson?"

"Yes, it was awesome! How much is Rags?" Laura asked intently.

"Don't worry about that now. We need to untack the ponies and put them away."

Mrs. Taylor quickly turned and headed to the barn with Pinocchio. Laura followed with Rags and put him in his stall.

"Let me help you," Pop-Pop suggested. "Unbuckle the throat latch under his jaw, and now the noseband under his chin. Gently pull the top of the bridle over his ears, and let the bit slide out of his mouth. Well done, Laura."

"Pop-Pop, isn't he perfect? Can we buy him?"

"Go talk to your mom and dad, and I'll put him out in his paddock."

"Okay! Rags, I love you so much," Laura proclaimed as she kissed Rags on the nose. Then she ran out to see her parents.

Rose and John were watching the mares and foals play together in a field dotted with buttercups, when Laura ran up from behind.

"Mom, can we buy Rags? He is really sweet! I love him!"

"It's a possibility; we are going to try. We need to see how much money we have, and Pop-Pop is going to call Mrs. Taylor in the morning."

"Oh, Mom, I have never been so happy! Thank-you so much for letting me get my own pony. I love you!"

"I love you too! Let's hope it all works out. We are going to head home and have supper."

They went to their cars after saying good-bye to Mrs. Taylor. "Look at her skipping! This is one of the best days I can remember!" John said, as he ran up, grabbed Laura, and threw her over his shoulder.

"I think we might have to get John a pony too!" Mom-Mom chuckled. "Have a good evening, Rose."

"I will call Mrs. Taylor in the morning and make an offer on Rags," Pop-Pop said as he hugged Rose good-bye.

"Thanks, Mom and Dad. I can't believe how excited I am!"

Chapter 5

Monday morning after breakfast, Pop-Pop got up quickly from the table and went to call Mrs. Taylor.

"Remember, if it's meant to be, it will happen," Mom-Mom said as she started to wash the dishes.

"Good morning. It's Jack Anderson," Pop-Pop said.

"I was expecting your call this morning," Mrs. Taylor replied.

"I wanted to talk to you about buying Rags. Would you take $850 for him?"

"No, I won't take any less for him. I have three other people who want to see him this weekend."

"If we gave you the full price, would you throw in a saddle and bridle?"

"I can't do that, but I can sell you his tack for $75," Mrs. Taylor said firmly.

Pop-Pop let out a big sigh and shook his head. "All right," he said at last. "So, it's $1,025 for everything?"

"Yes, and you couldn't ask for a nicer pony. Laura will be hard to beat at the fair this year."

"You have a deal. Could you deliver him this weekend?"

"Yes, but I need a hundred dollars to hold him."

"I will drop it off this morning."

"I will have the contract ready when you get here," Mrs. Taylor said in delight.

Mom-Mom was listening in the doorway as Pop-Pop went to his favorite brown chair, plopped himself down, and stared out the window. He looked at the empty fields that had once been filled with his beloved horses.

"Well...what happened?" Mom-Mom inquired.

"She's delivering Rags this weekend."

"Then what's wrong?" Mom-Mom asked.

"I think I've lost my negotiating skills. Mrs. Taylor drives a hard bargain, but I thought I could at least get somewhere. We are going to be $75 short if we get the tack."

"Don't worry about that. I have wanted to clean up around here. I'll sell my silver bowl above the fireplace."

"Your mother gave you that bowl! Are you sure you want to sell it?"

"I think she would understand. She wouldn't want Laura to have a pony and no way to ride him. I can take it to the antique shop this week."

With a sense of relief, Pop-Pop swiftly stood up and gave Mom-Mom a kiss on the cheek. "You're the best! Thank you! I can't wait until Rags gets here. I'll run the deposit over to Mrs. Taylor and stop by and see Rose. Do you want to come with me?"

"Not today. I wanted to start making my strawberry jam."

"I love your jam. I'll be back by lunch," Pop-Pop said as he quickly headed out the door.

Mom-Mom giggled to herself. "He's like a kid on Christmas morning!"

John had an early morning at work on Monday. The phone rang at three-thirty in the morning with the message that there was a car stuck on the highway. A single mother and her child had had a tire blow out and had run off the road. They were stuck in a deep ditch.

"Good morning, John!" Rose said when she stopped by to see him at the shop after dropping Laura off at school. "How did the tow job go this morning?"

"Not good. The winch couldn't pull the car out, so I had to pull it with the tow truck."

"Did you get it out?"

"Yes and I fixed the tire. Then I got them on their way."

"Oh, good. My mom called before I took Laura to school. She said Daddy was heading over to see Mrs. Taylor to give her a deposit. She wouldn't budge on the price, but they said not to worry, that they had everything covered. I can't wait."

With his head hung low as he sat at his desk, John replied, "Okay."

"Aren't you excited? What's wrong?"

Just then a very happy Pop-Pop came into the shop. "I just signed the contract and gave Mrs. Taylor a deposit. She is going to bring Rags to us Saturday afternoon. I need to go and pick up some hay for him this week. Did you tell Laura yet?"

"Yes, I told her on the way to school," Rose replied. She looked at her crestfallen husband. "John, what's wrong?"

"I've been sitting here for the past two hours trying to figure this out, but I don't know how," John said, while scratching his head. "Both of you should sit down."

Pop-Pop and Rose sat in the two chairs across from John's desk.

"What's going on?" Rose asked.

"John?" Pop-Pop added.

"When I pulled the car out this morning, a rod went through the engine block. I had to call a commercial tow truck to tow it here for me. It's going to need a new engine, there's no fixing the old one. I called around, and a new engine is going to cost close to $800. The company doesn't have that kind of money right now, and without the tow truck, I'm only going to lose business."

"Well, you *have* had a bad morning," Pop-Pop said, breaking the long moment of silence. "We can figure this out. How long will it be until the company has the money?"

"I called my buddy Butch, who always asks me about buying my '66 Ford pickup truck. He agreed to buy it if I can get it through Maryland State Inspection. I can have it done by the end of the week, and he said he could pay me the following week. That would be enough to cover the engine, but I can't wait that long to start fixing the tow truck."

"Are you sure you want to sell that truck? You have had it a long time."

John shook his head. "I do love it, but I have to keep the business going, and it will help us get Rags sooner."

"Well, there you go. I can lend you the money that I was going to use for Rags, and with your money, that should be enough. I'm sure Mrs. Taylor will hold Rags for an extra week, until you sell the truck. I'll stop by and see her on the way home. When do you need the money?"

"Dad, are you sure?" Rose asked, trying not to show her disappointment.

"Yes, I'm sure! I can drop the money off tomorrow morning, if that works for you?"

"That would be perfect! I can order the engine today, and it should be here tomorrow afternoon," John said with relief.

"I'll go talk to Mrs. Taylor on my way home. See you tomorrow."

* * *

Mrs. Taylor had just come up from the barn and was standing on her rustic covered porch when Pop-Pop arrived.

"Are you here for your lesson?" Mrs. Taylor asked coyly.

"Not today. I forgot my crop." Pop-Pop smiled. "I just went to see my son-in-law, and he had an unexpected business expense this morning. His tow truck needs a new engine. He needs the money now—the money we had set aside for the pony. He's going to sell another truck he has, and he'll have all the money by the end of next week. So, is next weekend okay with you?"

"I don't know, Jack. I have other people interested in Rags. The one lady might bring her trailer this weekend." Mrs. Taylor stared at the ivy that was entangled in the beams supporting the porch.

"I understand," Pop-Pop continued, "but it would mean a lot to me if you could hold him. Laura would be crushed if he was sold."

"I can't hold him that long when I might have someone willing to pay me cash this weekend. Rags could break his leg in the field next week, and then I wouldn't have anything. I'm sure that if he is sold, I can find something else for Laura. I'll go get your deposit," Mrs. Taylor said swiftly.

Pop-Pop stood on the porch speechless in total disbelief, and thought to himself, *I can't believe this woman. I thought she would understand!*

"Here you go, Jack," Mrs. Taylor said, handing him the envelope. "I'll call you Monday morning and let you know if he is still here. If he's sold, I know Laura will be disappointed, but it may be a good life lesson for her. You can't always have what you want."

Pop-Pop bit his tongue and nodded his head in agreement, not wanting to say what he was really thinking.

"Have a pleasant week," Mrs. Taylor said as she turned and walked away.

"I'm glad my mother taught me to be polite!" Pop-Pop mumbled to himself. "Laura is going to be crushed. How could Mrs. Taylor be so obstinate? If Rose sees her daughter upset, she'll never let Laura have a pony. I can't tell anyone, but I have to find her a pony before anyone finds out about Rags."

As he drove home, he thought to himself, *I'd better put this envelope in the glove box, so no one sees it. Where can I find Laura a pony cheap—the auction! It's this Saturday...*

Mom-Mom met him at the door. "Rose called and told me about the tow truck. Did you talk to Mrs. Taylor?"

"Yes. Everything is all set. I was thinking maybe Laura could spend the weekend with us, and we could clean up the barn for Rags. Saturday is the auction at New Holland. We could look for a saddle there, and it might be cheaper than Mrs. Taylor's."

"I think that's a great idea. I haven't been there in years, and I know they used to have a lot of saddles for sale at the auctions," Mom-Mom replied.

"Okay," Pop-Pop said, starting to worry. "But isn't this the Saturday the flea market is in town? I saw a sign on the way home. Why don't you and Rose go there? You know how long I like to stay at the auction. I would like Laura to experience the bidding and everything."

"I do like the flea market. I'll ask Rose if she wants to go. I'm sure John will be working," Mom-Mom said. "You aren't going to buy anything but tack, are you?"

"No, just tack. It's hard to find a nice pony at the auction anyway," Pop-Pop said with his face turning red. "What's for lunch?"

"Jack, there's something you're not telling me."

"I could never hide anything from you, could I? Mrs. Taylor wouldn't hold Rags. I'm afraid that if he is sold this weekend, Rose will change her mind. She doesn't want Laura to get hurt."

"Nobody wants to see Laura upset, but we need to prepare her in case he is sold. What were you thinking?"

"I'm not sure. I guess I was hoping to find her a pony at the auction."

"Jack, that's not an option. Finding a good pony there is like finding a needle in a haystack. If Mrs. Taylor sells Rags, then we will just have to wait to find the right pony. If it's meant to be, then it will be. Rose will be fine. She's not going to change her mind now. These things take time. I'll call Rose and let her know. I think you should go to the sale, though, and look for a saddle, but not a pony. I love you, Jack, and I understand. You just want Laura to be happy."

* * *

Rose got to school early, wanting to be first in line for pickup. The bell rang and Laura was the first student to exit the building. She saw her mom and rushed to the car.

"Hey, Mom. How was your day? Did Pop-Pop talk to Mrs. Taylor? Are we getting Rags?" Laura didn't allow time for Rose to answer any of her questions.

"Laura! Laura!" Rose pleaded. "Will you let me talk?"

"Oh, I'm sorry," Laura said.

"Yes, Pop-Pop talked to Mrs. Taylor," Rose said as she pulled out of the parking lot. "We are hoping to pick him up next weekend."

"Why can't we get him sooner? I don't think I can wait."

"Well…to be honest, your dad had a bad day today, and the tow truck needs a repair and he has to use the money for Rags to fix it. He's sold his red truck, and he is getting paid for it next week. Then, hopefully, we can get Rags. Mrs. Taylor has someone else coming to see him, and if he's not sold then, we can get him next weekend. If he is sold, Mrs. Taylor said she will find another pony for you."

"But I really want Rags!" Laura sobbed.

"I know, honey, but please try to understand. I need you to be tough so Daddy doesn't see you upset. He feels so bad about the money, but he doesn't have a choice."

Laura tried to stop crying. "I won't cry in front of Daddy. I know he doesn't want to sell his truck, either."

"It's fine, honey. He really wants you to have a pony. I think he's more excited than you are sometimes. Pop-Pop called and wants you to spend the weekend with them and clean out the barn. Then, Saturday night, he wants to take you to the auction to look for a saddle."

"That would be awesome! Are you going?"

"No, Mom-Mom and I are going to go to the flea market," Rose answered. "Let's stop by and see your dad at the shop."

When they pulled into the parking lot, John saw them and walked over to the car. He was anxious to see Laura. "Hello, beautiful. How was your day at school?"

"It was good," Laura answered as she wrapped her arms around his waist. "I heard you had a bad day?"

"It's all better, now that you're here." John kissed his daughter on her head. "I heard you are going to the auction on Saturday."

"I'm so excited! I can't wait!"

"Do you think there will be any boats there?" John joked.

"It's a *horse* sale, Dad!" Laura laughed. "Can you go?"

"No, I have to work." John put his arms around Rose and Laura. "Let's go home. I want to spend the evening with my two favorite girls."

John and Rose were sitting on the couch after Laura went to bed. "I'm a little worried about my dad going to the auction. I can remember when I was little. There was never a time when he didn't come home with a horse. My mom would get so mad. I think my mom even banned him from going at one point."

"But it must have been fun seeing all the new horses," John said.

"You would think, but some of the time the horses he bought were so sick that it would take months of care to get them healthy enough to ride. He felt so sorry for them. My mother would end up being the one taking care of the sick ones."

John leaned forward and said, "I can't imagine he would buy a pony there, knowing we are getting Rags, or another pony, from Mrs. Taylor."

Shaking her head and giggling, Rose replied, "John, you don't know my dad very well, but I hope you're right."

Chapter 6

Laura woke up very early Saturday morning at her grandparents' house. She ran downstairs to find Pop-Pop drinking coffee out of his favorite green cup.

"Good morning, Laura," Pop-Pop said.

Laura climbed into his lap and gave him a hug. She laid her head on his strong shoulders. "What time are we leaving?" she asked.

"Let's say around ten a.m. That will give us time to stop and eat lunch on the way."

Just then, Mom-Mom called them into the kitchen for breakfast. Laura hardly touched the pancakes and sausages Mom-Mom had piled high on her plate. After taking a few bites, she rushed upstairs to get dressed. She was so excited about the sale, she sat on the edge of the bed, thinking to herself, *I hope we find a saddle today!*

She heard Pop-Pop turn the ignition on the old Chevrolet truck, and she knew it was time to go.

Laura was running out the front door when she heard Mom-Mom ask, "Don't I get a kiss good-bye?"

"Oops, sorry!" She stopped in her tracks and gave Mom-Mom a kiss and a hug.

"Sweetie," Mom-Mom said, "remember—no buying a pony today! We want to have a Hadley pony!"

With a big sigh, Laura responded quickly, "I know, Mom-Mom, but it will be fun to look!"

"Laura, I told Pop-Pop the same thing! The two of you going to the auction together makes me very nervous," Mom-Mom said with a smirk.

Laura and Pop-Pop headed down the driveway. It was such a beautiful drive. The trees were at their peak of fullness. As they got closer to the sale, Amish buggies pulled by sturdy horses lined the side of the road. Laura looked at each horse with curiosity, wondering if they enjoyed their job.

Pop-Pop pulled into the diner parking lot where they were going to eat lunch. It was an old diner that he had eaten at for years. The Willow Diner was small, sparsely decorated with a few horse pictures, and it never seemed to change at all. But the home-cooked food was tasty and reasonably priced. They sat in a cozy booth facing each other and ordered lunch.

"Laura, I want you to eat all your lunch here. The food at the auction is not very good," Pop-Pop warned.

"Okay," Laura said. "How many horses do you think will be there?"

"Probably quite a few. This time of year, camps are looking for horses and ponies. Prices might be higher than in the fall. It's expensive feeding them hay all winter long. The dealers hope to make the money back at the auction," Pop-Pop explained.

"Who buys the horses?" Laura asked with much interest.

"It's hard to know who the buyers are. Some are looking for horses for themselves to trail ride, or to show.

Sometimes horse trainers buy them, hoping to get a bargain. They take them home and retrain them, expecting to make a profit by selling them for more money. Then there are the dealers, who will buy anything just to make money," Pop-Pop continued. "They usually own feedlots, where horses are kept in large groups, and small paddocks. It's a cheap way to care for them. The dealers keep them there and try to sell them to individuals or take them to a different auction, or they take them home and fatten them up. The horses are treated like inventory in a store, not like living animals," Pop-Pop explained. "We'd better get going."

There was no response from Laura as they left the diner and made their way back to the truck. She stared out the window of the vehicle and thought to herself, *One day, when I have my own pony, I'm going to keep it forever.*

It had just finished raining when Laura and Pop-Pop pulled into the auction about an hour before it began. There were horse trailers of all different kinds. Some were as big as tractor-trailers; others were just long enough for one horse. A few people were leading horses into the auction barn. There was a small riding ring where the horses could be tried out by anyone.

Laura and Pop-Pop parked the truck and headed to watch the action in the ring. The temperature had dropped after the brief rain shower, and it had become a bit chilly. This didn't help with the horses' behavior. The fresh, cool air had just started blowing across the ring, and like a chain reaction, the horses threw their heads back, snorted, and, in two instances, bucked their riders off! Laura and Pop-Pop leaned on the fence that enclosed the ring and tried to get a good view.

Chaos reigned. The two loose horses, feeling very fresh, bolted around as the other riders tried to control their mounts. Eventually, everyone decided to dismount and wait for someone to catch the mischievous horses. Soon everything settled down. Laura was mesmerized by all the activity and took it all in. She could have stayed there all day.

"We'd better get inside before we get too cold," Pop-Pop said. Laura didn't respond. She just turned and followed him into the sale barn. Pop-Pop knew his way around the barn, and he led Laura through the aisle where potential buyers and dealers were busy examining horses.

Pop-Pop stopped at the end of the aisle and started to talk with an old friend. As they talked, Laura watched the activity. The barn was old, with cobwebs lining the ceiling. The smell was strong of musky hay covering the floor with manure scattered all around. So many different noises filled the air. Horses, whinnying for friends they had been separated from, could be loud at times. A lot of chatter was going on between the dealers and potential buyers, whom they were trying to interest in their horses.

"This fine quarter horse gelding was shown all year by a ten-year-old boy. He won multiple year-end championships," one big-bellied dealer told a couple who was examining his horse.

The couple asked, "Why did they sell him?"

The portly dealer quickly explained, "After winter, the kid lost interest, so they called me, and I went and picked him up. You won't find a nicer horse anywhere."

71

Doubting the truthfulness of the story, the couple walked away. When a lady started to inquire about a different horse, the plump seller began to use the same sales pitch. Listening to the dealers' similar tales, Laura wondered, *Why are they here if the horses are so amazing?*

She soon began to realize that the dealers would tell the same story about different horses to anyone who showed interest. Laura started to tug on Pop-Pop's jacket, trying to get his attention.

"Are you okay, Laura?" Pop-Pop asked when he saw Laura dancing from one foot to the other.

"I really need to go to the bathroom."

Pop-Pop said good-bye to his friend, and they walked in the direction of the restrooms. There were so many horses and ponies in the aisle that they would walk ten steps, and then have to stop for a while. Not wanting to be separated from his granddaughter, Pop-Pop held Laura's hand firmly. The warm, tight grip made her feel secure.

"I'm doing my best to get you to the potty. Are you okay?" Pop-Pop asked.

"Yeah, I'm okay for now."

They finally made the turn into the side aisle where the bathrooms were.

The aisle was where the auction kept the ponies and young horses. The washroom was in their sights when Pop-Pop suddenly stopped in his tracks. He was staring at a small Shetland pony. She was covered in dry mud, with burrs in her mane and tail. He could barely see her face, but he saw her magnificent dark eyes filled with despair.

Pop-Pop quickly found a way to get Laura to her destination and he ordered, "Hurry up. There's a pony I want us to take a look at."

"What kind of pony?" Laura asked.

"Just go to the bathroom, and then I'll show you."

Laura hurried into the ladies' room while Pop-Pop stood guard at the door.

He looked at the pony and thought, *What a well-bred mare. That pony is too nice to be here.*

Chapter 7

Laura came running out of the washroom, hitting Pop-Pop with the door by accident. "I'm sorry. Are you okay?"

"I'm fine." Pop-Pop chuckled. "Let's go look at that pony."

They went to the aisle where the pony stood, head hung low, looking dejected. She appeared to be in rough shape and very displeased at being tied up beside larger ponies.

Pop-Pop carefully made his way past the bigger ponies while making sure to keep Laura safe.

He put his hand out, allowing the pitiful pony to smell him. Her velvet muzzle felt warm in his palm. He pushed her excessive forelock to the side, trying to see what was underneath. He saw the most beautiful dished face, with wide, somber eyes, and petite ears.

"Laura! Take a look at her," Pop-Pop said.

Laura slowly walked up to the pony, and the pony softly nickered to her in a quiet voice.

With an enormous smile, Laura said to the pony, "You are sweet. What are you doing here?" Laura gave her a pat on the neck. She was surprised to feel so much cold and hard mud caked on the miserable mare.

"She's a mess," Pop-Pop said. "This poor thing has been neglected for some time."

Laura found a brush buried in the musty straw next to the hayrack, and she began to groom her. As Laura moved the brush in a clockwise circle, the pony curled her lip in delight, closing her eyes, trying to enjoy the moment.

"She likes that," Pop-Pop noticed. "I'm sure it's been a long time since she has had any attention." As Laura brushed the mud away from the pony's coat, she could feel small, crust-like bumps under her hair.

"Pop-Pop, what's this all over her back?" Laura asked.

Pop-Pop took a look at what Laura had found.

"It's rain rot," he said. "That's what happens when a pony isn't brushed on a regular basis. Watch what happens when I pick it off. See the bloody spot? It can be painful to remove, and she has a severe case of it."

Just then, a grouchy-looking old man headed their way and saw them with the pony. "Can I help you?" he asked.

"Just taking a look at this pony," Pop-Pop said. "How old is she?"

"I don't know. Got her papers somewhere. She ain't much to look at," the surly man replied.

"Where did you get her?" Pop-Pop asked.

"A lady called me after her great-aunt died and needed to get rid of her. I picked the pony up this morning and brought her here. I think the lady was scared of her. She's probably afraid of her own shadow!" the miserable man said.

"I am Jack Anderson, and this is my granddaughter, Laura." Pop-Pop extended his right hand. "What's your name?"

"Don," he answered abruptly.

"You said she had papers. Could I take a look at them?" Pop-Pop asked.

"I think they are at the sales office," Don said. "The lady just paid me to haul her here. Doesn't matter much to me what this pony brings. It's cost more to bring her here than what she's gonna get for her. I've got a really nice lesson pony over here if you want to look at him."

"No thanks. We were just interested in this one," Pop-Pop explained.

"I think you are wasting your time," Don said as he walked away.

Laura and Pop-Pop looked at each other in confusion.

"He's not very nice!" Laura frowned.

"No, he's not. It's a shame we couldn't see the pony's papers before the sale starts," Pop-Pop remarked.

Just then, an announcement came over the loud-speaker, "The sale will start in ten minutes. We have eighty-seven head of horses to see today."

Pop-Pop took a long look at the pony, and noticed she was Hip Number Five. Every horse has a sticker on its hindquarters to identify it. And each horse took about one minute to sell.

She will be going through the sale in less than twenty minutes, he thought. *There's not enough time to take a look at her papers, or to see if she is sound. Mom-Mom will kill me if we bring her home, especially covered in rain rot!*

Gently petting the animal's face, Laura was reluctant to leave the pony's side.

"Laura, we should get a seat before the sale starts," Pop-Pop said. "What do you think of her? Do you like her? She's really gentle."

"I think she would be a perfect pony for me," Laura proclaimed.

"She looks really kind, but we don't know anything about her. Remember what Mom-Mom said? And we don't want to get a pony that isn't safe," Pop-Pop explained. "Let's go sit down."

"But, Pop-Pop, she shouldn't be here. I *know* she's a good pony—and she needs us!" Laura pleaded.

"Come on," Pop-Pop said firmly. "I'm sorry. We can't buy a pony we know nothing about!"

Laura gave the pony a hug and a kiss and whispered, "Good-bye." She could feel a lump in her throat as she walked away with Pop-Pop. They found seats at the top of the grandstand. The seats were made of wood, and they were not very comfortable.

There was a twenty-foot lane between rows of gates where the horses would trot back and forth and where the bidding took place. Various dealers leaned on the gates to have a closer look at the horses being sold. The auctioneer read a list of rules and terms before the official bidding started.

Pop-Pop leaned over and said to Laura, "Don't point at anything or raise your hand. The auctioneer will think you're bidding."

"I won't" Laura promised.

Pop-Pop could see the disappointment in her face, and he felt responsible for getting her so excited about the pony.

Hip Number One came into the sale ring. The bidding began, with the first horse selling for $225. The auctioneer started in on the second horse, which sold for $550.

"That was a nice horse, wasn't it, Laura?" Pop-Pop asked.

Laura pretended to be interested. "Yeah. He was fancy. I don't really understand the man selling them, or for how much. He talks too fast."

"That's what an auctioneer does. He tries to get you caught up in the moment, not giving you time to think. Just listen to the price he says before he drops the hammer to finalize the sale."

"I think I understand now."

As they were selling the third horse, Laura could see the pony she had brushed and with which she briefly had fallen in love. The pony looked so scared and worried, which caused Laura concern. She wondered where the mare would be going.

The fourth horse left the ring, after having been sold for $75. The auctioneer began to describe Number Five.

"Hip Number Five is a registered Shetland pony. She is eight years old. Her owner recently passed away, and the family doesn't know anything about caring for ponies."

The bidding started at $100, but since there was no audience interest, it quickly dropped to $50, and then to $25. The big-bellied dealer raised his hand, and then another dealer nodded his head. The bid was now at $55. Laura looked at Pop-Pop and gave him a nudge.

Pop-Pop was struggling with what to do. He wanted that pony as much as Laura did. Finally, without hesitation, he raised his hand and said, "Hold on. Can you tell me her registered name?"

Annoyed by the interruption, the auctioneer stopped and looked at her papers.

"Uh, looks like Hadley Spider," he responded, then proceeded with the sale.

Hearing the Hadley name, Pop-Pop and Laura looked at each other in pure shock. "Pop-Pop, we *have* to get her!" Laura quietly pleaded.

Without delay, Pop-Pop raised his hand and joined in the bidding.

The portly dealer also knew of the Hadley Pony Farm, and he knew that the pony was worth more than originally anticipated.

The auctioneer was at $82 for her, when the stout dealer raised his hand agreeing to the current price.

"How about $90 for this little darling?" the auctioneer asked Pop-Pop. Pop-Pop nodded his head accepting the price. As the next bid went to the other bidder, Pop-Pop thought to himself, *I only have a hundred dollars with me... I hope she doesn't go any higher than that.*

The bidding went back to Pop-Pop, and the price was now at $100. Pop-Pop had to think about it for a minute.

Laura saw the concern in her grandfather's anxious face, and asked, "What's wrong, Pop-Pop?"

"I only have a hundred dollars with me. I'm just worried I won't have enough money," Pop-Pop answered.

Laura's facial expression went from exuberance to total misery. Feeling helpless, Pop-Pop looked over at Laura, then agreed to the current bid. He knew that this would be the last bid he could place, and he waited to see if his opponent would outbid him. Pop-Pop wrapped his arm around Laura as they waited.

The big-bellied dealer took a moment to think about the price. When he looked up to see who the remaining bidder was, he saw a little girl filled with distress.

For a moment, he remembered being a young child, when he *really* loved horses, before they became just a source of income to him. Very briefly, he listened to his heart...something he hadn't done for a long time. He shook his head no and passed on the bid.

Hip Number Five. The warmhearted dealer glanced up at Laura, who was beaming with his decision. He winked and smiled at her. The joy he felt was worth more than money to him.

The auctioneer looked around to check for other bidders. Seeing no one else, he pointed toward Pop-Pop and dropped the hammer!

Chapter 8

"I can't believe we got her!" Laura whispered to Pop-Pop.

"She *is* ours. We'd better go pay for her," Pop-Pop said, "and then, we need to figure out how we are going to get her home."

Laura and her grandfather carefully made their way down the grandstand while the auction continued. When they saw the big-bellied dealer, Pop-Pop stopped and shook his hand.

"I wanted to say thanks," Pop-Pop said. "My name is Jack Anderson, and this is my granddaughter, Laura."

"You don't need to thank me. My name is Smoke Edwards, but everyone calls me Smokey," the dealer explained. "That could be a nice pony you bought."

"Hopefully, she is, under all that thick hair and crusty mud," Pop-Pop replied. "Guess we will have to wait until she sheds her coat to see what we have."

Trying to hide the real reason he'd stopped bidding, Smokey explained that the pony might have been too much of a risk for him.

"We'd better go to the sales office and settle up the pony. Have a good night," Pop-Pop said to Smokey.

"Thanks, and good luck with that mare," Smokey offered.

The men shook hands, and Pop-Pop started to head toward the office. "Come on, Laura," he said.

Laura looked up at Smokey and grinned with appreciation. Smokey gave her a tender pat on the head. Then Laura hurried along to catch up with her grandfather.

In front of them, horses were moving in and out of the sale ring and the crowd thickened. Dealers and buyers wove their way around long lines of hungry people queued up in front of food stalls. It would be a challenge just to reach the stairs leading up to the office, and those stairs seemed endless to Laura.

Pop-Pop finally reached the cashier; he was a bit out of breath and feeling overwhelmed as the reality of buying Hip Number Five began to sink in. It suddenly dawned on him that telling Mom-Mom about his pony purchase might be worse than he could have imagined.

The cashier handed Pop-Pop an invoice for the pony. "That will be one hundred dollars even, and here are her registration papers," she said.

Pop-Pop pulled out his wallet from his back pocket, took out all of the cash, and handed it to her.

After counting the money carefully, the cashier marked, "Paid in Full" on the invoice.

"Thank you," she said. "And remember, all animals must be removed from the premises by nine p.m. tonight. If you need to make arrangements for hauling, you can go to the stabling office."

"No problem," Pop-Pop said, knowing full well that he still didn't have a plan for getting the pony home.

Laura and Pop-Pop left the office and headed toward where the pony stood, waiting for them.

Laura could see her all alone, and the pony appeared to be filled with worry. But when she saw Laura, she picked her head up, pricked her ears, and softly nickered.

"It's okay, girl. Nothing bad is going to happen to you now. I will always take care of you," Laura whispered in her ear.

"What are we going to call her?" Laura asked her grandfather.

"Well, her registered name is Hadley Spider. Would you like to call her Spider?" Pop-Pop asked.

Shivers ran down Laura's back. She shook her head. "No! I am scared of spiders!"

Pop-Pop chuckled. "Well then, do you have any other ideas?"

Without hesitation, Laura said, "Let's call her Sugar, because she is so sweet!"

"That's perfect," Pop-Pop agreed. Then, in a more serious tone, he added, "We'd better find her a way home."

Pop-Pop knew that most horse shippers required to be paid up-front. He was hoping to find a person who would haul her home and accept payment when he dropped Sugar at her new home.

I have cash at the house, he thought to himself, *but I need to find a way home for Sugar right now.*

"Laura, stay here with Sugar. I'll be right back," he said.

"Wh-Where are you going?" Laura asked nervously.

"I need to arrange transportation for Sugar. I am just going to the stable office"—he pointed—"at the end of this aisle. If you need me, I'll be close by," Pop-Pop assured her.

As he started down the aisle, Pop-Pop was trying to ignore the churning of his nervous stomach. The reality of owning Sugar, needing a ride home for her, and breaking the news to Mom-Mom and the rest of the family had become unnerving. Seeing the glee on Laura's face as he looked back at her helped give him some peace of mind.

Laura was standing very close to Sugar, delicately stroking her cheek, when someone tapped her on the shoulder. It was Smokey!

"Didn't mean to startle you," he said. "Where's your grandpa?"

"He went to the stable office to find someone to help us take Sugar home," Laura answered anxiously.

"How far away is she going?"

"It's about an hour and a half away, I think," Laura explained, "close to Baltimore."

"No problem," Smokey said. "I can take her. I will go let your grandpa know."

Smokey was heading toward the stable office when Pop-Pop came out. Being unable to arrange transportation, Pop-Pop had tunnel vision, and he didn't see Smokey walking straight toward him.

"Jack!" Smokey called. "I was looking for you. I am getting ready to leave and could ship the pony for you."

With much surprise and relief, Pop-Pop answered, "That would be great! I am short on cash right now, but when we get there—"

Smokey interrupted him. "We'll worry about that later. Let's just get the pony loaded up. I drive a blue and tan Ford dually, with a beige six-horse gooseneck trailer. It's parked in the first row of rigs. I'll meet you there in twenty minutes."

"Did you buy any horses today?" Pop-Pop questioned.

"Nope, didn't see anything I liked, and I sold the two I brought with me. The pony will have the trailer all to herself. Hopefully, she won't get lost in there," Smokey chuckled.

"Sugar will feel like royalty," Pop-Pop joked. "We'll meet you at your rig."

Smokey went to the sales office to settle up on the horses he had sold. He was a regular at the sales event, and the cashier knew him well.

"Hey, doll, came to get a check for Hip Number Seven and Number Twelve," Smokey teased.

"Are you kidding?" the cashier asked. "The auction isn't half over, and you have never left without buying something."

"I need to help someone out," he explained.

"That's awful nice of you, Smoke," she said, handing him his check. "Have a good night. I'll see you next week!"

"We'll see…" Smokey replied. "Take care of yourself."

The perceptive cashier had a feeling that tonight might be the last time she would see Smokey at an auction. A few coldhearted dealers in the past had had a special moment in their lives, like Smokey had just experienced, that enabled them to feel true compassion. Once that happened, they could no longer be in the business of dealing horses.

Pop-Pop and Laura were heading to the parking lot with Sugar.

"I'll lead her to the trailer, Laura. I want to make sure she doesn't act silly," Pop-Pop explained at first. Then, later, he said, "Here, Laura, you can take her now." He handed her the rope. "She's not skittish at all."

Laura took the lead line in her right hand, gathering the extra line in her left hand. She was very careful not to wrap the rope around her hand.

"Good job, Laura." Pop-Pop smiled. "That's perfect, the way you're leading her."

"Mrs. Taylor taught me how to lead a pony when we worked with Rags," Laura told him.

Smokey was walking behind them, when he saw Laura leading Sugar.

"Hey, Jack," he hollered. "Do you see my rig?"

"Yes," Pop-Pop said. He waited for him, while Laura kept walking ahead with Sugar.

As the two men watched Laura leading Sugar, Pop-Pop put his hand on Smokey's shoulder and said, "Wish I had a camera!"

"You don't need one," Smokey said. "You'll have a snapshot in your head forever."

After Sugar was loaded into the trailer, they headed home. Smoke followed their Chevy truck. Laura didn't take her eyes off the trailer.

"You're going to get a stiff neck," Pop-Pop warned.

"Oh, Pop-Pop, I will be fine. I can't wait to get her home!" Laura proclaimed.

"I sure hope we're not in too much trouble when your grandmother sees Sugar," Pop-Pop shared.

Just then, the reality of having to tell Mom-Mom and her parents hit Laura, too. She turned forward and stopped watching the trailer. She just stared at the road ahead. She felt like she had swallowed a brick and it was sitting at the bottom of her stomach.

"Pop-Pop, do you think we're going to be in big trouble?" Laura asked apprehensively.

"I don't know, Laura, but I am pretty sure we won't be allowed to go anywhere without Mom-Mom and your parents with us from now on," Pop-Pop answered, trying to make light of the situation.

Seeing how worried Laura was, he added quickly, "It will be okay. They will love Sugar."

"Yeah, how could you *not* fall in love with her?" Laura reasoned.

As they made the turn into Pop-Pop's driveway, they could see the lights on in the house and Laura's parents' car. They glanced at each other at the same time, and were speechless.

Chapter 9

John, Rose, and Mom-Mom were relaxing at the kitchen table after dinner, just as Pop-Pop's truck and Smokey's truck and trailer pulled up.

"Mom," Rose said, "dinner was delicious."

"Thanks, dear. Would you like some coffee? It could be a long time waiting on Laura and your dad."

Then John, who was looking out the kitchen window at the long driveway, exclaimed, "Hey, I see headlights... I think they're home!"

"Laura is going to be tired tonight. It's been a long day," Rose remarked.

"I don't believe it!" Mom-Mom continued, changing her tone. "There's a truck and trailer following them!"

Mom-Mom and Rose stared out the window in disbelief.

"Come on, let's go see what's in the trailer!" John smiled, grabbed his jacket, and hurried outside.

Shaking her head, Mom-Mom looked at her daughter. "John is as bad as your father!"

Rose sighed and nodded. "John reminds me a *lot* of Daddy."

As Rose and Mom-Mom put on their coats, Mom-Mom became very quiet. She was thinking to herself, *I should have known better...letting them go to the auction without me... It wasn't a good idea.*

Rose could see the distress in her mother's face. She could remember, as a little girl, when Pop-Pop would return from auctions and sales with all kinds of destitute horses. Mom-Mom would be irritated at first, but after seeing the pitiful animals, she would always open her heart to them.

Deep in thought, Mom-Mom was sitting on the worn-out mahogany stool by the kitchen door, staring at the sink stacked with soiled dishes.

Rose prodded her. "Come on, Mom. Let's go see what they brought home."

Rose took Mom-Mom's hand and gave her a kiss on the cheek as they headed toward the barn.

"Laura, wait in the truck," Pop-Pop ordered. He parked on the grass next to the lane, hoping to make room for Smokey's huge rig. Smokey pulled up next to Pop-Pop's truck and turned off the clanging diesel engine.

Pop-Pop went into the barn, trying to find the lights. It took a while for him to make his way through the maze of cobwebs that lined the deserted stable. Pop-Pop wiped his face, and flipped the switch. The lights blinked on and off until they warmed up. The barn appeared to be completely coated with filthy cobwebs.

Smokey walked into the aisle and bellowed, "What a mess! Guess nothing has been living in here for a while."

Smoke found a broom and began clearing a path into the first stall on the right.

"It's been about five years since I've even been in here," Pop-Pop said. "After we sold the last horse, it made me heartsick to see the barn empty."

"I can only imagine," Smokey said as he willingly continued to tend to the unlivable stall.

Sugar started to become restless in the trailer all by herself and started whinnying, hoping to hear a familiar voice. When there was no response, she became silent.

"Go help Laura with the pony, and I will finish the stall," Smokey suggested.

Pop-Pop nodded and moved quickly toward his truck. As he approached it, he noticed John was just reaching the barn.

John had a big smile on his face. "What did you bring home?"

"John, you wouldn't believe it if I told you," Pop-Pop answered. "Here—look at the papers." Pop-Pop pulled the documents out of his shirt pocket and handed them to John.

"Dad, she's a Hadley pony from Mrs. Taylor's farm!" Laura blurted out before her father could open the envelope. John was very surprised to hear the Hadley Farm name. Mom-Mom and Rose also were close enough to have heard Laura.

"Did you say it's a Hadley pony?" Mom-Mom questioned.

As soon as Laura heard Mom-Mom, she turned and ran over to her grandmother and her mom, wrapping her arms around Mom-Mom and nestling her head in her grandmother's cozy coat.

"She's a real Hadley pony, Mom-Mom! Her name is Sugar!" Laura announced. "Come on." Laura gestured to her mother and grandmother. "Let's go see her!"

Laura took Mom-Mom's hand and grabbed Rose's jacket. Sugar's excited new owner directed the two of them to the back of the horse trailer.

Pop-Pop and John followed behind the ladies. Hearing the discussion, Sugar began to chatter again. Pop-Pop opened the large back door of the enormous trailer. Staring back at them was a very needy pony.

"It's okay, girl. You're home now," Laura coaxed her. "Isn't she the most beautiful pony ever?"

"Oh my goodness," Mom-Mom said, catching her breath. "That sorrowful, dear old pony needs some tender loving care!"

With much relief, Pop-Pop put his arm around Mom-Mom. "I knew you would understand why we couldn't leave her at the auction."

"We'd better get her in the barn. She's had a long day," Rose suggested.

Sugar was relieved to be out of the trailer. She looked around at her new home and made a loud sigh. Then she lowered her head and began to eat the lush grass at her feet.

"She seems right at home," Smokey declared as he stepped out of the barn.

"I would agree with that." Pop-Pop nodded. He began to introduce Smokey to the family.

"Thanks for bringing Sugar home. You have made our little girl very happy." John started to reach into his back pocket, pulling out his wallet. "How much do we owe you for the hauling?"

"Ten bucks will be fine, and I'll throw in a bale of hay," Smokey stated.

"Are you sure?" Rose asked.

Feeling a little uneasy, Smokey declared, "Ten dollars is all I will take. I should probably get going. I have a busy day tomorrow."

Shaking hands, John gave Smokey the ten dollar bill. Smoke set fresh hay on top of the old, unusable bales in the aisle of the barn.

Smokey walked over to Laura, patted her on the head, and said, "Take care of that rain rot. Good luck with her, kid."

Much to his surprise, Smoke felt a warm rush as Laura's little arms wrapped around his plump middle.

"Thanks again, Smokey—" Pop-Pop began, but Smokey waved him off. "Yeah, well, gotta go," he said, scurrying to his rig. He jumped in and drove toward the house to turn the trailer around. As he passed Pop-Pop's family, waving good-bye to him, Smokey couldn't control the immense smile that covered his face. It had been

a while since he had felt a part of something this mean-
ingful and important.

"Come on, Laura," Mom-Mom said. "Let's put Sugar
in the barn. We need to get both of you to bed. Tomorrow morning we need to start working on the rain rot,
and Sugar sure needs a good grooming."

Laura carefully led Sugar into the barn, making sure
she found her a bucket of water. Pop-Pop brought in two
small flakes of the fresh, soft hay Smokey had left for her.
He placed the hay in the corner of the stall, next to her
water bucket.

Sugar lowered her head and dragged Laura over to the
tasty hay. The pony quickly grabbed a mouthful and
began chewing in delight, closing her eyes and trying to
savor every strand.

"I think it's been some time since she's had decent
hay," Rose stated.

"Pop-Pop, can she have more?" Laura asked.

"No. Too much rich hay could make her sick."

Laura took the pony's halter off and went to stand with
her parents, as they watched Sugar peacefully eating.

"I made an apple pie earlier today," Mom-Mom announced. "Who would like a slice?"

"That sounds wonderful," Rose replied.

Laura went over to Sugar and whispered in her ear, "See you in the morning. I love you, Sugar."

Laura headed out of the stall as Pop-Pop secured the door and turned out the lights. John challenged his daughter, "Laura, race you to the house?"

Laura nodded and immediately darted up the driveway.

Watching Laura and her dad race to the house, Mom-Mom nostalgically thought to herself, *They remind me so much of Pop-Pop and Rose, when she was Laura's age.*

"We need to get home," Rose said. "John is ushering at church in the morning."

"Mom, Dad, may I spend the night at Mom-Mom's?" Laura pleaded. "I need to make sure that Sugar is doing all right in the morning."

Pop-Pop assured Laura's parents, "We can get up early and meet you at church."

"Of course," John answered. "Your mother brought church clothes for you just in case you were late coming home."

"We have to get up around six a.m. Sugar is going to need a lot of attention. I can remember, about twenty years ago, a horse that was covered with rain rot like Sugar. It took nearly three months to get him healthy."

After Laura finished her dessert, her parents headed home. Laura went upstairs and took a long hot shower.

Pop-Pop came upstairs to say good night to her. She climbed in the tightly fitted sheets, and Pop-Pop tucked the handmade quilt over her.

"Are you tired, sweetheart?" Pop-Pop asked. "You're awfully quiet."

"No, I'm just worried about Sugar," Laura conceded.

"She'll be okay. It may take a little time, but we'll get her all fixed up." Pop-Pop smiled.

Laura continued, "I really wanted to start riding her…"

"Laura, we don't know if she is even broke to ride," Pop-Pop explained. "You need to get some sleep, young lady. We can worry about this tomorrow. I love you, and good night."

Pop-Pop kissed her on the forehead and whispered, "You're the reason Sugar is in the barn tonight." As he headed downstairs, Pop-Pop reflected, *I feel alive again!*

Laura lay in bed fretting and thinking to herself, *I hope I can ride her soon! I really want to go to the State Fair with her and win the trophy!*

Chapter 10

Mom-Mom was the first one up on Sunday morning, even before the sun rose.

She came down the steps very quietly, trying not to wake Laura or Pop-Pop. She made her way to the kitchen and clicked on the coffeemaker. While her beloved coffee brewed, she began to peel potatoes for breakfast. Mom-Mom's home fries were Laura's favorite part of the morning meal. Mom-Mom placed the freshly peeled potatoes in her lime-green bowl and added some cold water. Then, with much anticipation, she poured herself a cup of fresh coffee and sat at the antique kitchen table, under the bay window. Mom-Mom watched the sun rise, and there was enough light to see the silhouette of the barn.

I hope Sugar was okay last night. She certainly has been through a lot, and being all alone in the barn doesn't help, Mom-Mom thought. *Ponies don't like living by themselves; they can become depressed. We have a lot of work to do, trying to clear up that atrocious fungus!*

Mom-Mom stood up quietly from the table and set her coffee carefully on the kitchen counter. She then began to collect the supplies they would need to take care of Sugar's rain rot. She placed the baby oil and Listerine on the mahogany stool by the kitchen door.

Just then, Laura entered the room, startling Mom-Mom. "Good morning, Mom-Mom," she said as she stretched her arms.

"You sure are up early, young lady. Are you anxious to see your new friend in the barn?"

"May I go check on Sugar *before* breakfast?" Laura begged.

"Of course, but first go upstairs and get dressed, and wake up Pop-Pop," Mom-Mom insisted.

"Yes, ma'am!" Laura turned and flew up the stairs.

"Is the house on fire?" Pop-Pop joked as he met her near the top.

"Mom-Mom said I could go down to the barn to see Sugar!"

"You'd better slow down a little," he suggested. "I will meet you downstairs." The smell of simmering bacon led him to the kitchen.

"I think you're the best cook on the East Coast, and I was smart enough to marry you," Pop-Pop bragged as he wrapped his arms around Mom-Mom.

"You have always been a charmer." Mom-Mom chuckled. "I have everything you need for Sugar on the stool by the door. Take them down to the barn. Try to rub her down with the baby oil. That will loosen up the scales and make it easier to pick them off. Then we will use the Listerine to clean up Sugar's skin."

Just then, Laura ran back into the kitchen. "I'm ready!" she declared excitedly.

"Get your boots on, young lady, and we will go see how Sugar did last night," Pop-Pop said, smiling.

"Don't be long," Mom-Mom fussed. "We need to eat breakfast and get to church on time."

Pop-Pop and Laura went to the barn. Pop-Pop gently tugged on Laura's long ponytail and commanded, "Whoa—Pony!" Laura looked up at Pop-Pop, and the two began to laugh.

They walked into the dark, lonely barn, and when Sugar heard them, she started to nicker. She was very happy to have company. Sugar met Laura and Pop-Pop enthusiastically at the opening of the stall door.

"She's feeling better!" Pop-Pop observed.

Sugar, in her excitement to see her new owners, and trying to get out the door, almost ran over Laura.

Laura smacked Sugar on the shoulder and held her ground. "No! Sugar!" she scolded. "You need to wait!"

Sugar quickly backed up and stood quietly in the stall.

"Well done, Laura," Pop-Pop praised. "That's just the way to be the boss. You can tell that Sugar knows better. Someone has taught her manners in the past, but it's very important that she respects you."

"Good girl, Sugar," Laura said, as she patted the pony's neck.

"We'd better rub her down with the baby oil, then get up to the house for breakfast. When we get home from church, you can take her out for a walk, and let her graze for a while," Pop-Pop explained.

"Can I rub it on?" Laura asked.

"Sure. Here you go." Pop-Pop handed her the oil.

"Should I pour it on or put it in my hand?"

"Just put it in the palm of your hand and start near her withers. You know, the highest point on her back, and work your way down. Don't get right behind her. Stay on her side so you don't get kicked," Pop-Pop instructed.

"Is this good?" Laura asked as she began to spread the oil on Sugar's loose winter coat.

"That's perfect!" Pop-Pop chuckled as Laura became covered in pony hair. "It looks like we have two ponies now!"

"This is messy!" Laura said, trying to get the hair out of her mouth. "I'm going to have to take a bath before church."

It took almost half of the bottle to cover the rain rot. When they were finished, they swiftly headed for the house.

After church, Mom-Mom, Pop-Pop, and Laura went to the barn to continue treating the fungus. As Mom-Mom picked at the large chunks of scabs, Sugar's raw skin, underneath, began to bleed. With every tug, Sugar would pin her ears and drop her back in an effort to avoid the pain.

"This is worse than I thought." Mom-Mom sighed. "She may need a vet and antibiotics."

"Will she be okay?" Laura asked, with concern.

"She should be fine," Mom-Mom answered. "It's just going to take some time for her to heal, and the medicine will make sure it doesn't get any worse."

Laura thought, *I hope Sugar heals soon. I can't wait to start riding her.*

"I will call Dr. Hall in the morning," Pop-Pop promised. "It's been a while since I have seen him..." Then he put his arm around Laura. "Your grandmother is a wonderful nurse."

With a chuckle in her voice, Mom-Mom clarified, "I don't know about that, but I think Sugar has had enough of me picking the rain rot for today. Laura, let's take her out for some grass."

Laura led Sugar to the lush, green meadow across the driveway from the barn. When Sugar saw the thick, green grass, she lowered her head and made a beeline for the spot, dragging Laura with her. When they reached the mouthwatering meadow, Sugar immediately dropped her head and began eating.

"They look content," Mom-Mom said to Pop-Pop, as they watched Laura and Sugar.

"I think, when the vet comes, he should worm her. She looks like she has a wormy belly, too. I know she's sweet, but I hope we can get her straightened out," Mom-Mom said with concern.

"I noticed her big belly, too. It looked worse after Laura groomed her, and you can see more of her under all the hair. It could take a couple of months to get her healthy," Pop-Pop said.

"Jack, I understand why you bought her, but this may not be the best pony for Laura. She obviously has been neglected. Who knows if she's even broke? Let's see what the vet says and how much the bill will be for him. Maybe, if Rags isn't sold, we can still get him, and then decide what to do with Sugar," Mom-Mom said in frustration.

"I know that Rags may seem like the ideal for her, but I have a feeling Sugar is the right pony. There's just something special about her. She has the kindest eyes I have ever seen. Trust me, everything is going to work out," Pop-Pop declared as he motioned for Laura to bring Sugar back to the barn. "I'm going to walk around the pasture to check the fence with Laura, and then we can turn Sugar out. John is going to help me, if we need to repair any fence, when they come to pick up Laura."

"I hope you are right," Mom-Mom said as she headed up the driveway. "I'll be in the garden if you need anything."

"Is Mom-Mom upset?" Laura asked as she put Sugar in the stall.

"Maybe a little. She's just worried and wants to make sure Sugar is the right pony for you. Let's not think about that now. We need to walk the fence line to make sure it's safe."

"Yes, sir. What should I do?"

"Follow me and look for nails sticking out on the boards. We don't want her to get cut by a nail. Then we will walk to the pasture and check for gopher holes. She could accidently step in one and break her leg."

With a hammer and nails, Pop-Pop and Laura walked the entire field, fixing half a dozen boards. Laura walked the field from one end to the other, looking for any holes.

"I think that will do it," Pop-Pop said. "I think we can turn her out. Did you find any problems?"

"No, just found a couple of big rocks. I threw them under the fence. Should I go get her?"

"Yes, let's turn her out for a couple of hours. Before you let her go, walk her around the fence line so she sees everything. I don't want her to be so excited to be out that she runs into something," Pop-Pop instructed.

Laura led Sugar around the entire two-acre pasture. The small stream that divided the field was deeper than usual, and Laura found rocks to step on to cross without getting wet. Sugar was hesitant to follow and planted her feet, refusing to get them wet. Laura tried to coax Sugar, and then pulled her with all her weight. Without any warning, Sugar leaped into the air, jumping the stream as if it was a three-foot jump.

She landed on the other side and looked back at Laura, who was lying on the ground, covered in mud from head to toe.

"Are you okay?" Pop-Pop asked, as he ran over to check on Laura.

"Yes, I'm fine. Just a little dirty," Laura replied as she sat up and started to brush herself off.

Sugar walked over to Laura, pushing her with her nose. "I think she's sorry." Pop-Pop snickered. "I think she's seen the whole field, so go ahead and let her off the leadline. I think we need to get you cleaned up before your parents arrive."

Laura released the snap under the halter and let Sugar free. They headed to the gate with Sugar following close behind. She stared and watched them through the gate as they walked away from her, and started to whinny.

"I don't think she likes being alone," Pop-Pop said as he looked back at the pony.

"I know I wouldn't want to be alone," Laura said as she slowly walked in her heavy mud-spattered jeans. "Can we get her a friend?"

"Let's wait and see what the vet says."

The following Monday morning, Pop-Pop and Mom-Mom were finishing breakfast and enjoying their coffee when the phone rang.

"Hello?" Pop-Pop answered.

"Hi, this is Lisa from Dr. Hall's office returning your call about a Shetland pony," the receptionist stated. "Dr. Hall could see her at four p.m. today."

"That's perfect," Pop-Pop replied. "Thanks for your call." Pop-Pop hung up the phone and called Rose to let her know the time.

Laura and her mom arrived at Pop-Pop's at 3:45 p.m., not wanting to miss Dr. Hall's visit.

Pop-Pop had Sugar out eating grass. Laura jumped out of the car as soon as her mom parked.

"How's she doing?" Laura asked. "Hi, Sugar! I missed you."

"I'm doing fine, too, thanks for asking..." Pop-Pop joked.

Just then, a substantial green truck with a white vet box in the back pulled into the driveway. When the truck stopped, a very tall, rugged-looking man stepped out.

Laura thought, *That's the tallest person I have ever seen!*

"Jack Anderson, it is sure nice to see you," Dr. Hall stated. "That is the cutest pony I have seen in a long time."

Pop-Pop motioned to Laura to bring Sugar back to the barn.

"Thanks for fitting us in, today," Pop-Pop said. As the men shook hands, Pop-Pop continued, "Sure is nice to see you."

Laura led Sugar back to the barn. The two men were catching up on old times, as Dr. Hall took supplies out of his truck.

"Lisa didn't tell me what you needed today for the pony," Dr. Hall said. "By the looks of her, you're going to need to know when the baby is due."

"Uh…no…" Pop-Pop started. "I thought she had a bad case of worms, but now that you mention it, she does look pregnant!"

Chapter 11

D r. Hall finished his initial exam of Sugar and went out to his truck to get the antibiotics.

"Laura, I'll be right back," Pop-Pop said. "Start trying to comb out her mane with that blue comb in the bucket. I am going to pay Dr. Hall and get her medicine."

"Here is sulfa trim for the fungus. Give her five, twice a day for ten days. I will recheck her then and see how she's doing," Dr. Hall instructed. "I didn't want to say anything in front of Laura, but she's in foal. She's already started to bag up. I think she's going to foal within the next month or so. It's hard to tell because she's under-weight, but I would keep a close eye on her."

"Do you think she'll be okay?" Pop-Pop asked.

"I hope so, but I'm concerned. I don't like how thin she is, and with you buying her at the auction, she could have been exposed to strangles or shipping fever. The next ten days will show if she picked up anything at the auction. Keep a close eye on her, and take her temperature every day. Call me if you see a runny nose, cough, or if she stops eating. With the rain rot, keep it clean and put Destine on it, and that will help keep it from getting re-infected. I think, with diligence and keeping a close eye on her, we might be okay."

"I sure hope she's okay. I haven't been to a sale in a long time. I didn't think about her getting sick," Pop-Pop said as he watched Dr. Hall write up the bill. "What about the foal?"

"If she doesn't get a fever, the foal should be fine. Hopefully, she wasn't bred to anything too large. It's hard to know how big the foal will be, and whether she will have trouble with the delivery. You can call me anytime if she starts to foal. I would feel better being here in case she gets into trouble." Dr. Hall handed Jack the bill. "You can mail the check to the office. Do you have any questions? I'm not trying to scare you, but I'm a bit worried about her."

"No, I don't have any questions now. I would hate to see something happen to her as attached as Laura has become to her. I guess I shouldn't have bought the pony," Jack said, leaning on the truck with his hand over his face.

"I understand, but I know if anybody can help her, it's your wife. She's one of the best caregivers I have ever seen. Could you get Laura another pony, and that way she has something to have and ride? It could be quite a while before Sugar can be ridden."

"Mrs. Taylor has one we have been looking at, but I just need to figure out the money. Her ponies are very expensive. The money I've spent on Sugar didn't help, either."

"Why don't you call her and explain about Sugar? She may know some of the history about where she was, and who she was bred to. Don't worry about my bill now. We can always work that out later. I would rather

Laura have that pony first. You were always good to me, and I missed seeing you after you sold out," Dr. Hall explained. "Well, got to go, or I'll be late for my next appointment."

Pop-Pop watched Dr. Hall drive away. *I don't know what I was thinking,* he thought. *I hope I haven't made the biggest mistake of my life. I can't believe the bill is so high. Over sixty dollars. It would be almost impossible to have enough money to buy Rags now.*

Pop-Pop made his way back into the barn and heard Laura talking to Sugar as she combed her thick mane.

"Laura, I have her medicine. I'm going to go to the house to get some applesauce to mix with it."

"Why do you need applesauce?" Laura asked.

"It's an old trick to get Sugar to eat her medicine without her knowing. I'll dissolve the pills in water, then mix it with applesauce. Sugar will think she's getting a treat!"

"You are so smart!" Laura declared.

"Thank you, but I'm not sure about that," Pop-Pop joked. "I'll be right back."

Pop-Pop walked into the kitchen, where Mom-Mom and Rose were snapping fresh green beans.

Rose looked up. "What did Dr. Hall say?"

Pop-Pop walked over to the table and sat down across from them. He scratched his head and after a long pause said, "Well, it looks like we will be having two ponies soon. She is in foal, and he thinks she could foal within a month."

The ladies looked at each other and began to laugh in delight. "That's exciting! Did you tell Laura?" Mom-Mom asked.

"No, I want to call Mrs. Taylor first and see if I can find out a little bit more about Sugar."

"Mrs. Taylor left a message on the answering machine today. I must have been in the garden. She said Rags was still available—the other lady couldn't make it. We could pick him up this weekend, if we want," Mom-Mom said.

Pop-Pop sighed. "I think I made a mistake buying Sugar. Dr. Hall is really worried about her. The fungus is going to take a while to clear up, and she could have been exposed to shipping fever at the sale. Hopefully, the foal will be okay. It could be a long time until she can be ridden."

"Dad, I think she'll be okay. Buying Sugar wasn't a mistake. We can all pitch in and get her fixed up. Don't be so hard on yourself!"

"Thanks, Rose. That means a lot," Pop-Pop said as he held her hand. "I'm going to go call Mrs. Taylor. Where are the papers from the sale, Virginia? I haven't had a chance to go through them yet."

"They are right next to your chair, in a folder," Mom-Mom said.

Pop-Pop opened the folder and began to shuffle through the papers. He saw her American Shetland Pony Association registration papers, and then the Coggins test that was required by the state to check for a mosquito-transmitted disease called EIA. He put all those papers to one side and then found what he was looking for: a small slip of paper. It was a stallion certificate, stating that Sugar had been bred to Hadley Zeon.

"Look at this!" Pop-Pop exclaimed, as he walked into the kitchen waving the paper. "Sugar was bred with one of Mrs. Taylor's finest stallions. This foal could be really nice. I'm going to call her now."

He quickly made his way into the living room, plopped himself down in his chair, and picked up the phone.

"Mrs. Taylor, it's Jack Anderson."

"Oh, good. I left you a message earlier today. The lady can't come until the first of the month. If you still want Rags, he's yours."

"Well, I'm not sure. I took Laura to the auction this weekend, looking for a saddle, and we bought a pony—" Pop-Pop said.

Mrs. Taylor interrupted. "I'm surprised you would buy a pony from a sale. You know everyone just unloads the bad or sick ones there," Mrs. Taylor said in disgust.

"I know, but this pony was special. She's a Hadley pony. Her registered name is Hadley Spider. The dealer who had her said the owner had died and her niece didn't know what to do with her."

"Oh my goodness. I had no idea that Mrs. White had died. She bought Spider from me as a foal. She's one of the nicest ponies I have ever bred. I had her here all last summer; used her for camps, and bred her to Zeon. Is she in foal?"

"Yes, just had the vet here. She's covered in rain rot, thin, and looks like she could foal in the next month or so."

"That poor thing, she is so sweet. I can't thank-you enough for getting her from the sale. Would you want to trade her for Rags? Jodi, my granddaughter, has always wanted her, since she broke her. I would love to give her to Jodi. I won't let Jodi keep a gelding, because they can't have babies." Mrs. Taylor chuckled.

"Really, are you sure?" Pop-Pop hesitated. "She's in rough shape."

"Yes, I would love to have her back. Do you want me to bring Rags down in the morning and I can pick her up?"

"That would be great! I can't wait to tell Laura! Thanks so much. I'll see you in the morning." Pop-Pop smiled as he hung up the phone.

He came into the kitchen, grabbed the applesauce, and started out the door, without divulging any information to Mom-Mom or Rose.

"Jack, Jack!" Mom-Mom said. "What did Mrs. Taylor say?"

Pop-Pop appeared startled. He stopped and leaned back in the doorway. "Sorry, I was so excited! Mrs. Taylor wants to trade even for Rags. She's bringing him in the morning and picking up Sugar."

"What!?" Rose and Mom-Mom said at the same time.

"She wants Sugar back for her granddaughter, Jodi, and Laura can get Rags. This is perfect. We won't have to worry about Sugar's health, and Laura could go to the fair this year! I feel so relieved. I was so worried that I made a big mistake. It's all going to work out!" Pop-Pop exclaimed.

"Hold on, Jack Anderson! You are not the only one making the decisions around here. Laura loves that pony in the barn. Don't you think we should ask her what she wants? Mrs. Taylor is a very smart businesswoman. She must know how nice Sugar is, and she doesn't give away *anything.* I think we need to have Laura's input on this, too!" Mom-Mom argued.

"I already told Mrs. Taylor to come in the morning. I can't change my mind now. Laura will want Rags," Pop-Pop said, defending his decision.

"Dad, you will give Laura a chance to have a choice. If there was a choice when Trigger got hurt, that he could have lived but never been ridden again; I would never have wanted to get rid of him. He was more than just a pony to ride—he was my best friend.

"Laura knows in her heart who her best friend is going to be, and she needs to be the one to choose. Daddy, you're always trying to fix everything, like when you bought me another pony without asking me first. I needed time to cope with losing Trigger, and then I might have wanted a new pony, but you never asked me what I wanted. I know you meant well, but you can't protect us all from getting hurt. I guess I'm a lot like you!" Rose said as she embraced her dad. "Let's go ask Laura what she wants."

"I'm sorry, Rose. I just wanted to stop you from hurting," Pop-Pop replied. "You are right about Laura. Let's go see what she thinks. Will both of you come with me?"

As the threesome entered the barn, they could hear chattering coming from Sugar's stall. They stopped and listened to the conversation.

"Do you like your hair done this way?" Laura asked Sugar. "Tomorrow I'll bring my box of ribbons, so you can be extra beautiful."

"I'm back, Laura. Sorry I took so long," Pop-Pop announced, not wanting to startle her. "I have the applesauce. She looks lovely! You have been hard at work on her."

"She does look gorgeous!" Mom-Mom said. "Pop-Pop talked to Mrs. Taylor about Sugar."

"What did she say?" Laura asked.

"Well, she said that she would like to have Sugar back," Pop-Pop answered. "I didn't tell you earlier, but Sugar is going to have a foal. Dr. Hall thinks in the next month she will foal."

"A baby? Oh my gosh! I am so excited," Laura exclaimed.

"I know having a foal would be exciting, but it can be risky. She could have some problems foaling, and the vet is concerned about her health. She could get sick from being at the auction, and he thinks it could be a while before you can ride her," Mom-Mom explained. "The good news is that she is broke and has even been used for camps."

"I don't care about riding her. I will take care of her—and the baby. She will be fine," Laura pleaded.

"Laura, I know you would do that, but Mrs. Taylor would be willing to trade Rags for Sugar. She would like to have Sugar for Jodi," Pop-Pop said. "You could go to the fair this year on Rags."

"Sweetie," Rose said as she sat on the hay in front of Laura. "It's your decision. Whatever you decide, we will support you. What pony do you want?"

Laura was speechless. She stared at Sugar, as everyone was waiting to hear her decision, trying to be patient.

Laura took a deep breath and said, "I love them both. When I rode Rags it was awesome. I thought about taking him to the fair, since I rode him. Sugar needs me, and I love her, but I really want to ride. I don't know what to do."

"Laura, I want you to have a special pony like I had with Trigger. Laura, who do you think could be your best friend?" Rose asked.

"Oh, that's easy. I know who that is," Laura said with much relief. "I have made my decision!"

Chapter 12

"What time do you think Mrs. Taylor will be here?" Mom-Mom asked.

"Any minute," Pop-Pop said. "She was going to head over here once she finished her morning chores. I'm going down to the barn now. Are you coming?"

"Yes," Mom-Mom said. "I wouldn't miss it."

Just then, they heard the sound of Mrs. Taylor's diesel truck and the clanky stock trailer it hauled, slowing down and turning onto the driveway. The red truck's loud diesel engine roared as Mrs. Taylor steered it to a parking spot beside the barn. When she cut off the engine, the faint sound of a whinny came from the trailer. Sugar perked up and neighed when she heard it.

"Good morning, Jack and Virginia," Mrs. Taylor said as she shook Pop-Pop's hand. "I have the pony for you. Can I see Spider before I unload?"

"Sure, follow me," Pop-Pop said, as he headed into the barn and over to Sugar's stall. "We have been calling her Sugar. Laura doesn't like spiders, so she can't bring herself to call her that."

"Sugar is a great name for her. She does look rough. It's so sad that she was neglected after Mrs. White died. Last year, in the middle of summer, she was stunning. Her coat shined like a new penny, and her dapples stood out like I have never seen before. Her mane, when it's washed, will be pure white. Are you sure you won't change your mind?" Mrs. Taylor begged.

"No... Laura won't part with her. I appreciate your offer, and I'm sorry that I agreed to the trade before I talked to Laura," Pop-Pop explained. "Virginia has the money for Missy. I can't thank you enough for selling her to us. I know Sugar will love the company."

"Here you go, Mrs. Taylor," Mom-Mom said as she handed the money to Mrs. Taylor. "Two hundred and fifty dollars."

"Perfect. Here are her papers," Mrs. Taylor said, as she pulled the envelope out of her dress pocket. "She will be one on August eighteen. Missy looks very weedy next to the other yearlings, but I think it's just because she's the youngest. We'd better get her off the trailer, so I can get back to the farm."

The wide door swung open, and a very tiny pony looked back at them. Mrs. Taylor led her off the trailer, and she leaped down onto the pavement, causing her to slip. "Be careful, little one," Mrs. Taylor said to Missy.

"She's a beautiful chestnut, and I love her cream-colored mane," Mom-Mom said.

"Here you go," Mrs. Taylor said as she handed Jack the lead rope. "Have fun with your new ponies. If you ever change your mind, I'll buy Sugar at any time. I can't tell you how much Jodi wants to own Sugar. I bet you're going to have a spectacular foal. Call me when she has the baby. Well, got to go."

"Mrs. Taylor, we are very sorry about Jodi," Mom-Mom said. "I hope she understands."

"Trust me, I understand. Jodi is a tough kid, and I will find her a pony." Mrs. Taylor smiled and climbed back into the truck.

Pop-Pop led the new and frightened pony into the barn as the trailer pulled away. He put her in the stall next to Sugar and let her have the freedom to explore her new world. Missy reached her tiny nose through the bars to meet her new companion.

"I wish Laura could be here," Mom-Mom said as she watched the ponies. "I love it when they seem like they are whispering to each other in pony nickering. I'm going to get Laura's room ready. She'll be out of school for the summer on Friday. I'm so excited that Rose and John agreed to let her stay with us until the foal is born."

"I am, too. It's going to be a great summer. Is Rose bringing her today to see Missy?"

"No, John is bringing her tonight. Rose has a church meeting."

"I'll wait till tonight to feed them, then. I'm going to turn Sugar and Missy out together for a while and then clean the stalls."

"Do you need help?" Mom-Mom asked.

"No, I'm good." Pop-Pop led the two ponies toward the pasture.

"Okay, I'll be up at the house." Mom-Mom smiled and headed up the driveway.

Pop-Pop led the two ponies into the large meadow and turned them to face the gate. He let them go, and leaned on the gate, putting one foot on the lower fence board. As he watched them walk away, it seemed as if they were Velcroed together.

I could watch them all day, Pop-Pop thought. *I don't think I've been this happy in a long time.*

That evening, Laura came running into the barn to see the newest pony.

"I just brought them in, after being out all day," Pop-Pop said. "Here's Missy. Isn't she cute? She's petite for her age, but I think she will catch up, with time."

Laura slowly entered the stall and carefully tried to touch the skittish yearling. Missy stretched her short neck toward Laura, to investigate the newest person in her life.

"Where's the new boat?" John loudly joshed as he walked toward the stall, startling Missy and causing her to move away from Laura.

"Dad, you need to be careful around Missy," Laura instructed. "She's pretty nervous around new people. She's so tiny, but it looks like Sugar loves her."

"Sorry, didn't mean to scare her," John apologized. "She seems nice."

"It's okay, Dad," Laura said as she shut Missy's door and went into Sugar's stall. "I sure missed her today."

"She's doing great. She has no fever, and she is eating all the feed I give her." Pop-Pop sighed. "We should feed them dinner, and I think Mom-Mom will have dinner ready for us soon."

Laura started to mix Sugar's feed, as Pop-Pop prepared Missy's dinner. The two ponies whinnied with excitement, anxiously waiting for their food. As quickly as their meals were delivered, they were gone. Laura gave them each two flakes of hay, as Pop-Pop brought them their water.

"Sugar's appetite is great," Pop-Pop said as they walked to the house, "That's a good sign that she is not going to get sick."

* * *

The last day of the school year had finally arrived, and Rose was the first in line to pick up her daughter.

"Yeah, I thought the day would never end," Laura announced as she climbed into the front seat. "My friends in school want me to write them when Sugar has her baby. All of them gave me their addresses before I left. Everyone was so nice today."

"I'm so happy to hear that," Rose said, as she drove toward her parents' farm. "How is your report card?"

"It was good: one A, three Bs, and one C."

"Great job, Laura. Your dad is going to be very happy to hear that. I am so proud of you!"

"Thanks, Mom. Did you bring my suitcase?"

"Yes. It is in the trunk. We sure are going to miss you. Hopefully, Sugar will have the baby soon."

"I am going to miss you, too, but I can't wait to spend the night in the barn."

"I hope your grandfather is up to it. He's not as young as he used to be," Rose said, "but I have to admit, I think the ponies are making him feel younger."

* * *

Laura reluctantly organized her temporary room at her grandparents' place, wishing she could stop and run down to the barn.

"Are you finished yet?" Pop-Pop hollered upstairs. "We need to feed the ponies."

"Almost," Laura said, as she put her last pair of shorts in the drawer.

"Jack, don't rush her," Mom-Mom fussed. "I told her I want that room to be kept nice and tidy."

"All done," Laura said, as she flew down the stairs. "I'm ready!"

At the barn, Pop-Pop and Laura only saw Missy standing. Sugar was nowhere in sight. They quickly began to search for her and found her lying flat and motionless under the large willow tree at the far end of the pasture.

"Come on, girl, get up," Pop-Pop encouraged, as he tried to get her to her feet. "I don't think she feels very good. Laura, get her halter and shank."

"Is she okay?" Laura asked nervously.

"I'm not sure. Be careful that Missy doesn't get out when you open the gate, and hurry!"

Laura ran as fast as she could, climbing the fence instead of opening the gate. She grabbed the halter and shank, and made her way quickly back to Sugar, who had just stood up on her own.

"She's up. Let's get her into the barn," Pop-Pop urged. He led the weary pony to her stall. "Put Missy in her stall, and then bring me the thermometer," he said.

Pop-Pop carefully tied Sugar to the stall door and began to examine her, as Laura looked on anxiously. He pressed his ear up to her belly, listening for gut sounds. Then he took her temperature. He flipped her upper lip and examined her gums; checking for good color. And he peeked at her udder to see if milk was coming in.

"Her temperature is normal, and I can't find anything wrong with her," he said. He let Sugar go. "Go ahead and give her dinner, and, hopefully, she'll eat it."

Laura quickly made up Sugar's dinner and served it. She put the grain in the feed tub, and showed Sugar where it was. Missy whinnied for hers, with much anticipation, but Sugar looked at her food, and turned away, hiding in the corner.

"Do you think she's sick?" Laura asked.

"I'm not sure. I don't think she's colicky, which would be like a bad stomachache. She has gut sounds, so I'm confident her stomach doesn't hurt. Her temperature is normal, so I don't think it's shipping fever. Her gums have good color, which is a good sign. Her udder isn't full, so she's not close to foaling yet," Pop-Pop explained. "I'm going to go to the house, call Dr. Hall, and get your grandmother. Can you watch her? If she lies down, don't let her roll. Okay? I'll be as fast as I can.

"We will be fine, Pop-Pop," Laura said, as she stroked Sugar's neck.

Pop-Pop raced to the house and thought, *We should have gotten Rags, and let Mrs. Taylor take care of Sugar. This is too stressful.*

"Do you have a headache, Sugar?" Laura asked her as she combed through Sugar's mane with her fingers. "Look at Missy. She can't stop staring at you. She's worried, too! Let me get you an apple, it's from my lunch. I saved it for you. Take a bite, and I'll give some to Missy."

Sugar refused the apple and became restless. She kicked at her belly, and looked at her sides.

I'd better go get Pop-Pop, Laura thought. *But what if she rolls while I'm gone? I can't leave her!*

"Sugar, don't lie down, please," Laura pleaded, as she watched Sugar lie down in the deep straw bed. "Okay, girl. Don't roll. Just lie still."

The distressed pony lay flat on her side, and began to groan in pain. She picked her head up, looked at her hindquarters, and then rested for a moment, only to repeat this several times.

Laura stayed close to Sugar's face, caressing it, when she lay still. The sound of water pouring onto the straw confused Laura.

"I wish Pop-Pop was here," Laura said as she watched Sugar helplessly.

All of a sudden Sugar lifted her head, and with the loudest groan, squeezed her belly, and out slid a tiny foal, covered in a wet film. Sugar laid her head back down in exhaustion, and the foal lay there motionless.

"Sugar, you did it!" Laura exclaimed. She got up to take a closer look at the foal.

The foal showed no signs of life, and Laura looked on in despair. Missy was watching the foal, too, and began to paw at her stall door; trying to get a closer look.

Laura was very stressed with Missy banging on the wall and the foal not moving. She leaned down to examine the foal more closely and realized that its nose was covered by the sack it had been born in. She could not breathe. Laura quickly removed the slimy cover from her nose and began to rub her. Suddenly, the foal stirred, and within a couple of seconds, she became very lively.

"You scared me, little one," Laura scolded the new life. "I'm glad you're okay. Look, Sugar, at your beautiful baby."

Sugar slowly stood and turned around to meet her daughter. She licked her all over, as the wobbly baby attempted to stand up.

"Laura, how is she doing?" Pop-Pop said, entering the barn. "Dr. Hall is on his way."

Pop-Pop and Mom-Mom peered into the stall and were shocked to see the foal.

"Sugar had her baby," Laura announced as she proudly showed them the foal. "Isn't she beautiful? She didn't move at first, but then I took that yucky stuff off her nose, and she was fine."

"Unbelievable," Mom-Mom said. "You delivered your first foal by yourself. Laura, I'm so proud of you! You're an amazing little girl."

"You did a great job," Pop-Pop added. He praised Laura and went into the stall to get a closer look at the new addition. "Let me take a look at you, little one. It's a girl, and look at those markings. She's a pinto, with four white stockings and a wide blaze. I think she's going to be chestnut and white. She's perfect! I couldn't be happier with her. I am so proud of you. Were you scared?"

"I was terrified, and I couldn't move at first," Laura explained, "but then Missy started banging, and that's when I realized I needed to wipe her nose off. I think Missy might have helped me save her."

"She must have known you needed help," Mom-Mom said, as she put her hand through the bars to scratch Missy's nose. "She's a keeper, for sure! I'm going to go call your parents and tell them the exciting news."

Within an hour; Dr. Hall, Rose, and John had arrived to see the baby. Everyone was watching Sugar and her foal getting to know each other, when the little one leaped in the air out of pure excitement. She had learned to use her legs and wanted everyone to see her many talents.

"Sugar certainly tricked us, but she has plenty of milk. That's one athletic foal. I think she's pretty special," Dr. Hall observed. "What are you going to name her?"

All the adults looked at Laura, waiting to hear if she had a name for the baby she had saved.

"I'm going to name her Hip Hop!" Laura giggled.

"I love it, Laura!" Mom-Mom smiled.

"This is way better than winning the trophy at the State Fair!" Laura announced, turning to look at them all. "This is the best day of my life!"

Follow HipHop as her adventure continues and find HipHop Merchandise at

www.HipHopTails.com

Also Follow her on

FaceBook -Hip Hop Tails
@hhtails

Instagram-hiphoptails

Don't forget to join the club!

CPSIA information can be obtained
at www.ICGtesting.com
Printed in the USA
BVOW03s0042041116
466923BV00001B/3/P